# Twice Born

## Other titles from INDIAN WRITING

*Krishna Krishna* by Indira Parthasarathy

*Star-Crossed* by Ashokamitran

*I, Ramaseshan* by Aadhavan

*Love and Loss* by Jayakanthan

*A Home in the Sky* by Vaasanthi

*Once an Actress* by Jayakanthan

*Wings in the Void* by Indira Parthasarathy

*Rishi Moolam* by Jayakanthan

*Paper Flowers* by Aadhavan

*Today* by Ashokamitran

*The Temple Elephant* by P S Sri

*Into This Heaven of Freedom* by Indira Parthasarathy

*Where the Lord Sleeps* by Neela Padmanabhan

# Twice Born

Vijay Raghavan

INDIAN WRITING

**Twice Born**

A novel in English by Vijay Raghavan

Pages 200, Price Rs 200

Indian Writing - 13

ISBN 978-81-8368-469-9

An Indian Writing publication
Published in India by New Horizon Media (P) Limited
33/15, Eldams Road
Chennai 600 018, India
Phone: +91-44-4200-9601/03/04
Fax: +91-44-4300-9701
Email: indianwriting@nhm.in
Website: www.nhm.in



First published in 2007

## About the author

Vijay Raghavan has been a professional journalist for three and a half decades. Starting in 1972, he has worked in newspapers in the four metropolises: Mumbai, Delhi, Kolkata and Chennai. He has worked for four major newspaper groups: *Indian Express, Anandabazar Patrika, The Hindu* and *Times of India*. He has been a business journalist since 1975, but has covered politics too, including the Lok Sabha between 1985 and 1988. He was editor of the website *chennaionline.com* and has helped launched Indian language websites like *webulagam.com* and *weblokam.com*. For five years, he wrote a weekly humour column called 'Cross Connections' in *Business Standard*, the financial newspaper of the Anandabazar Patrika group. For four years, he wrote a weekly column on the editorial page of *The Hindu* called 'A look at the economy'.

To my wife Tanaya,
daughter Lavanya and son Vivek

Part I

# The Conquest of Unhappiness

# Chapter 1

*'That that is, is. That that is not, is not. That that is both is a human being.'*

—'The Collected Aphorisms of the Unknown Punter', an unpublished existentialist Tamil classic by a Chennai householder.

I became we at seven o'clock on the longest day of the year at the moment when the ancient wall clock bonged for the seventh time.

In the bathroom I placed the razor at the joint on my jaw where lathered cheek began. Hand steady but razor in trembling stasis, I stared at my face, nut brown and sudsy white. I saw myself and behind me I saw my self.

There is nothing mystic or metaphysical about what I have said. It is the literal truth. I saw two of me, the second showing clearly through the first; and then I saw more of me, more and more, stretching out into the immeasurable spaces beyond the bathroom mirror. Have you ever been in a barber's saloon where the seats face away from each other and there are mirrors on opposite walls? You see yourself in the mirror facing you and in that you see the reflection of your image in the mirror behind you and so on in infinite progression. It was something like that.

It was no hallucination. I was filled with a deep intuitive knowledge that I had attained the secret ideal of many in the twenty-first century after Christ: I had become a schizophrenic. I knew that my realisation was real because I felt godlike, two-in-one, the mind and its familiar, the Creator and the Created in one entity. One and infinity packed in a tachyon.

The razor swooped, ripping and slashing and goulashing, the day-old beard. I felt intensely alive, liberated. And thus uplifted on the wings of self-realisation, I sang:

*'Twas brillig and the slithy toves*

*Did gyre and gimble in the wabe;*

*All mimsy were the borogoves*

*And the mome raths outgrabe.*

Ah, Charles Ludwig Dodgson, (Lewis Carroll to those of you who do not read Readers' Digest) you knew that there is more nonsense in heaven and earth than that is dreamt of in our philosophy. And talking of nonsense, does it make sense, you may well ask, for me to immediately decide that I had become a schizophrenic? Could not my experience have been something mundane; like a momentary blurring of the vision that uncoalesced the singular into the plural?

My psychiatrist asked me the same question when I talked to him later. Yes, I know that anyone who goes to a psychiatrist ought to have his head examined, but this shrink is an old friend; we used to bunk school together and go swimming in the Marina pool in Madras. Telling him about my new state of bliss was more an act of faith in an old friendship than a desire to be treated and cured. I like being a schizo. It is more fun being a mental Rubik's cube than an intellectual amoeba.

As I said, my psychiatrist friend Sankaran Nair, who has studied under that great German mindbender, Dr Gesundheit Scheisskopf, asked me the same question. That was because he knew, as well as I did, that I distrust the intuitive, the mystical, and the non-rational. I am a beef-eating Brahmin and my soul (not that I have one or believe that others have souls, but it seems to be the best portmanteau word to describe the essence of an individual) is closer to that of my friend Mehboob Sheriff, the porcipophagic Muslim, than that of my grandfather—who lived and died as a priest in a small temple in an insignificant village in the Thanjavur district of Tamil Nadu.

I am not like the hundreds of millions of my countrymen. To me, the fakir and the faker are indistinguishable. To most Indians, the supernatural is as real as the material. To them the tales of the soul of the mythical king Vikramaditya occupying other bodies are as believable as those of the local landlord jumping from wife to second wife to mistress to concubine. Such tales evoke in me not awe or benign acceptance but savage laughter.

I remember a bit of doggerel I wrote some years ago when a three-year-old Spanish boy called Ozel was brought to Delhi. The capital went into a tizzy when the boy's parents, and diverse religious cranks, claimed that Ozel was the reincarnation of a Tibetan lama named Yeshe, who had died decades ago. The poem ran thus:

*I sing the tale of the little lama.*
*He came with his papa and his mama.*
*Dogs at the lamp-post and the bored newshound*
*His skipping soul did amaze and astound.*
*Disarmament and Gorkhaland,*
*Rajiv Gandhi, the foreign hand,*
*Budget blues, the Punjab drama*
*Lost out to the toddler lama.*
*Editors yelled: 'You, you and you*
*Run out and get an interview*
*With Ozel, the baby lama.*
*If he's mum, talk to his mama.'*
*Reporters ran, cameras flashed,*
*But the lama sat unabashed.*
*Milk bottle he sucked or his thumb*
*Deaf to praise or opprobrium.*
*Newsmen and women went gaga*
*When the lad said 'ba', they cried: 'Wah!*
*How ineffable, how profound';*
*Their eyes went rolling round and round.*
*The kid gurgled 'goo', they went 'Ooh,*
*There's lama Yeshe peeping through*
*Death's dark, impenetrable veil;*
*Hail the reborn lama, all hail.'*
*If what they say of him is true,*
*I wonder who, I really do,*

*I was in my previous janma,*

*A sinner or a mahatma?*

*Was I Keats or Napoleon,*

*Bismarck, Lenin or Lord Byron?*

*But I know that with my karma*

*I was only a dumb llama.*

You get the picture? Yet, Sankaran Nair had a point I suppose because, the moment I saw my several selves in the mirror, I not only decided that I was a schizophrenic but also allowed my mind to spout metaphysical mishmash like the many-in-one, and the intermingling of infinity and eternity. But Nair, you see, is sane and therefore by the lights of human thinking, rational and thus cannot realise there are certain questions that Man cannot ask. I am not talking of hoary old chestnuts like 'When did time begin?' and 'Does the light shine in the refrigerator when the door is closed?' I am talking of unaskable questions like 'What did the monkey say, pissing in the moonlight?' Of course I know the answer to that and so must you if you are half-way educated. If the passage above does not convince you that I am crazy, the rest of the book will.

Nair would have made a lot more sense if he had asked me whether I thought there was any connection between the fact that I became a schizophrenic at seven in the morning, and the fact that I was using a Seven o'clock blade at that moment. Ah! There is a question worthy of a giant intellect capable of infinite dissection: a problem like those the Christian theologians of the dark ages debated for centuries—'How many angels can dance on the head of a pin?'

Is there something significant in the fact that I was using a Seven o'clock blade when I went schizo? Maybe there is, maybe there isn't. Maybe the answer lies in the nature of time, which is supposed to play funny tricks when something is travelling at the speed of light. Ask Einstein, ask anyone. Thought, it has been postulated, travels at the speed of light. This postulate can be proved thus: the time taken for the human brain to translate Bo Derek's basketball breasts into a jocks-imprisoned erection, is the time taken for light to travel from the cinema screen to the young man's eye. This is an empirical truth. Therefore, it is acceptable to postulate that there might have been a splitting of reality between seven a.m. and the Seven o'clock blade, as my thoughts sped at 186,000 miles per second from the images in the mirror to the realisation of self-realisation. You can explain anything anyhow, and there will be people to believe you. Ask Hitler and Goebbels, ask Senator Joseph McCarthy, ask Josef Stalin, ask Golwalkar and the Shahi Imam of Jama Masjid.

Or maybe, there wasn't anything significant. The universe is full of strange coincidences which, we have been told, will not be inexplicable when man attains certain attributes: the same attributes that he has gifted to his creation, the Creator. Can we read any meaning into the fact that a crone in Lithuania farted when Boris Yeltsin hugged Bill Clinton on television? Maybe we can, maybe we mustn't. Maybe it was her version of the raspberry; maybe she had violated the Pythagorean interdiction and eaten too many beans for dinner; maybe her rear was echoing a tremor in the cosmic flux, set off by an atavistic memory of how Brahman rippled, when the boom of Om sounded the birth of creation. I don't know. Neither does me. I am schizophrenic, remember?

But this I do know. By the way, I will be using I, we, and they interchangeably to mean me. If this confuses you I apologise; you'll just have to get along as best you can. Or you could just throw this book into the wastepaper basket and curse the blurb writer who conned you into buying it. Now, where was the we/I/us/them/they/ourselves? Oh, yes. But this I do know: the doctors won't believe me when I tell them that I attained schizophrenia at precisely seven in the morning. No, they won't tell me my clock was running fast or that I incorrectly heard seven bongs instead of eight. They will tell me it is impossible for a man to become a schizophrenic within a split second.

Got it? Ha, ha, ha, ha. Do I hear laughing groans? I remember a science fiction short story by Isaac Asimov which postulated that the pun is the only human type of humour; the other forms of funniness have been implanted in us by a superhuman race of aliens who are using us as experimental material, just as we stick needles into the brains of rats. And why can't this be true? The pun is the only form of humour that provokes groans, the opposite of laughter; paradox is the only truth. So the punster is the only true human wit. Why am I spending so much of my energy and your time analysing a lousy joke? Because comedy is too serious a matter to be taken lightly.

And then, I am trying to understand what has happened to me. I have been divided into many personalities.

Let me quote Arthur Schopenhauer: 'In every case, laughter results from nothing but the suddenly perceived incongruity between the concept and the real objects that have been thought through it in some relation.... All laughter therefore is occasioned by a paradoxical and hence unexpected subsumption, it matters not whether this is expressed in words or deeds.'

Incongruity, paradox, inconsistency, stultiloquy, double entendre, ambiguity, spinosity, dichotomy, enigma, steganography, and dilemma—all these words have acquired crucial significance for me now. (I admit I peeked at Roget's Thesaurus before writing that sentence.)

I remember Gautama, the Buddha, exclaiming: 'How can anyone laugh who knows of old age, disease and death?' O Bodhisattva, you got it all wrong. How can anyone not laugh who knows of old age, disease and death? The tragic is funny; switch off the sound in your TV set, the next time you watch boot-blacked Laurence Olivier declaim 'Put out the light and then put out the light' and see how you laugh. See, even Willie the Bard could not resist the pun in one of his most tragic scenes. And isn't it tragic that I have gone funny in the head?

# Chapter 2

*'What we observe is not Nature itself, but Nature exposed to our method of questioning.'* —Werner Heisenberg

But then, is it really tragic that I have become a schizophrenic? On reflection, perhaps not. For instance, I realised, in the brief time between soaping my legs and shouting to my wife Jenny—she is my second wife, the first one was a Grade One bitch who did not give me the satisfaction of kicking her out because she divorced me first—to get me a towel, that I had been granted a marvellous opportunity to study the workings of the human mind. The scientific method, my tenth class teacher told me, lies in breaking up things to see what is inside. We are all scientists up to the age of eight. That's why toys never last more than a day.

When I was a whole personality, I could not understand, most of the time, what the hell I was doing. The misogynist really wants to screw the brains out of every woman he meets, but he does not know it. How can he? How can he attain self-realisation, when he is a personality integrated by the apparently single emotion of disliking the female sex? How could I apply the scientific method to myself when I was a single entity? Now I had two or three or four of me to work on, for schizophrenia really means a splintered personality. A wealth of scientific research material had been created for me; an increase of several hundred percent in a nanosecond! I could visualise a tremendously exciting future, a lifelong study of my several selves. I would astound the world with my insights. Roll over Freud, Lie down Laing, here comes Bharat Sharma.

And who, you may ask, is this Bharat Sharma? He keeps popping up like the nauseating commercials during the live telecast of the Augusta Masters! My apologies. Bharat Sharma is me. I should have introduced myself earlier.

*Abhivaadaye!* I salute you! Descended from the three Rishis Angirasa, Puruhutsa and Traasadas, belonging to the Shatamarshana Gotra and the Bodhaayana Sutra, a student of the Yajur branch of the Vedas, I am, sir, Bharat Sharma.

Now do not ask me to explain what Gotra is or what Sutra means, and let me make it clear once and for all that I wouldn't know the Yajur Veda from the dimples on Dolly Parton's now steatopygous buns. I was born a Brahmin you see, and this is how my ancestors, going back perhaps five thousand years, have always introduced themselves to their elders. I was taught to do it the same way when the priests slung the sacred thread across my shoulders at the age of eight. I got a fit of the giggles when the priest made me repeat the millennial introduction and my uncle slapped me hard, to make me behave like a true and serious Brahmin. My mother cried and I bawled and my father consoled me with an ice-fruit, after which I concentrated on what the priest was intoning. I learnt it so well that I can recite it still, despite banishing my Brahminism the day I destroyed God, after reading Bertrand Russell's '*Why I am not a Christian*'. That was the day I lost my sacred thread swimming in the Cauvery with my grandfather, who lived and died on its banks in Thanjavur district. I was 14 years old that day and I am now 48.

If I were finicky about titles, I would call myself Dr Bharat Sharma. I did for a while, after I got my doctorate in English Literature 22 years ago. It was the first flush of priggish self-congratulation. Since then I have been a lecturer in a college, a public relations manager in a bank, a teacher again, a clerk in a shipping company and am now a reporter for the Madras edition of the *Indian Herald* newspaper.

Those who like me, call me Bharat; those who do not, like my ex-wife, call me a 'Thanjavur Paapan'. Literally the label means, a Brahmin whose origins are in the Thanjavur district of Tamil Nadu, but figuratively it is like an onion; layer upon layer of meanings and associations—a few of them complimentary, most of them pejorative and some vitriolic. The term is applied to an individual of a none-too-attractive sub-culture, a mutated and stunted remainder of the Brahmin caste of ancient India. The vast intelligence watered down over the millennia, so that it is the cunning sub-plot that attracts the mind, not the grand design. The Thanjavur Paapan is still very intelligent with usually a mathematical bent of mind, and the arrogance and selfishness which are the natural children of the cold intellect. But his vision is narrow, satisfied as he is with small gains, willing to be undernourished with watery

Vatha Kuzhambu (the poor man's version of sambar) and dry, roasted pappadams. This is for the few rupees saved by not using pulses and oil, which can be hoarded to give his daughter a wedding sari (with a few more microns of zari than the one which Shivasubramania Aiyar next door gave his daughter). And a dash, or rather a liberal helping, of acidic sarcasm and biting hurtful wit; a passion for intrigue within and outside the family; casteist bigotry that will allow only a Brahmin inside the kitchen; an obsessive and paradoxical code of cleanliness that does not allow a son to brush against his mother before he has bathed, (the mother has to bathe again to cleanse herself from the impurity passed on by her unbathed son). While the children are encouraged to shit on the road; a religiousness that masquerades as philosophy and oneness with Brahman, does not allow a Harijan of the lowest caste to draw water from the same well. And, voila! You have the Thanjavur Paapaan.

Or, is he, just another human being?

Now, allow me to leave you for a while. This is the prolegomenon and there will be a short interval, followed by some diversions and interludes, as the set is changed behind the curtain. Ice-cream and popcorn are on sale on the other side of this page.

But before we part briefly, let me leave you with another question that may or may not be asked:

*Tell me, should I, when I grow old*

*Wear the bottoms of my trousers rolled?*

Think about it. The answer is on Page 127. No, no, don't peek. Ha, ha, you peeked didn't you? The answer is elsewhere. Wait and wonder.

# Excerpts from 'Les Cahiers du Bharat Sharma'

(But first, by way of explanation, a quote from John Steinbeck's *'Sweet Thursday'*: In the prologue, Mac says: 'Sometimes I want a book to break loose with a bunch of hooptedoodle. The guy's writing it, give him a chance to a little hooptedoodle. Spin up some pretty words maybe, or sing a little song with language. That's nice. But I wish it was set aside so I don't have to read it. I don't want hooptedoodle to get mixed up in the story. So if the guy that's writing wants hooptedoodle, he ought to put it right first. Then I can skip it if I want to, or maybe go back to it after I know how the story comes out.')

Long ago, a friend of mine went to Delhi to work as a journalist. He was young, only 24 years old. He had a degree in economics from Madras University and a two-year diploma in journalism. He was equally well-versed in Vedanta and Marxist theory. He was idealistic; he wanted to reach the unreachable star of doing an honest job as a newspaperman.

He thought he could do it. In fact, he was positive he could perform a vital role in society of informing and educating the public and thrilling them and his peers with his investigative exploits. He was just like you and me at the age of 24.

My friend thought he had gone to Delhi at the right time to realise his dreams. It seemed to him (as it did to seven hundred million other Indians like us) that the age of corruption of body and soul and mind, had ended. A brave new world promised to come into existence, the cowardly old one ready to be washed clean by Youth.

We all know what happened. My young friend is now an old, old 32. He is as cynical as I am, which is saying a lot. He is as cynical as another friend of mine, a senior assistant editor, which is saying even more.

I met him recently when he came to Chennai on a holiday. He was down with a serious attack of Delhibellyache and had come down south to seek spiritual solace. Fat chance.

He showed me a poem he had written the previous year, when he was approaching the terminal stages of soul cancer. I give it to you as a gift. He called the poem 'Bitter Chocolate'.

*I've decided to rejoin the human race,*

*Now that I live in Connaught Place.*

*I'll not wear my heart on my sleeve.*

*Once more the tangled web I'll weave.*

*Now that I've rejoined the human race*

*My psyche will I interlace*

*With that of a trader in Chandni Chowk:*

*I'll sell only pigs in a poke.*

*Now that I live Connaught Place,*
*Before my peers I will lose face*
*If, at the bus stop, I do not outrun*
*The kakopygous Delhi matron*
*Long, long ago I did strive to see*
*I did unto the others as I would unto me;*
*But now I'm human and can see properly*
*I'll do unto others before they do it to me.*

# Chapter 3

*Love is, chatting at breakfast*

—'The Collected Aphorisms of the Unknown Punter'

After bathing, I reached into my wardrobe and threw on the first ironed pair of trousers and khadi kurta that I could find, and went into the kitchen where Jenny my love, my wife, was getting breakfast ready.

She was at the stove, scrambling eggs. I stood behind her, pressed my groin against her beautiful buttocks, slipped my arms around her and gently squeezed her bountiful breasts. Jenny lifted her hands, placed them over mine and squeezed. This is a daily ritual we go through. Most days, it ends with my giving her a quick kiss on the neck and moving away to the kitchen table where we have our breakfast. Sometimes, we let the eggs burn and the toast char and slide back to the bedroom for slow, gentle love-making. Joy cometh in the morning.

That day, I prolonged the kiss on the neck, gave her an extra squeeze and moved to stand next to her. She went back to stirring the eggs and I stared at her right ear, willing her to turn and look at me. Of course, it didn't work. She picked up the saucepan, slid the scrambled eggs on two plates, placed them on the table, sat down and started buttering slices of toast. I sat on a chair facing her and looked at her.

Jennifer Sharma nee Jones was 35 years old. She had the body of Marilyn Monroe, the quiescent, submerged sex appeal of a Bengali film star, the sensitivity of a poet and could have found a job as a chef in any five-star hotel. So why hadn't a man grabbed her, married her, fathered five sons from her by the time she was 25? Because her face was her misfortune; her DNA had moulded her face more along the remembrance of her horsy British subaltern grandfather and thick-lipped, flat-nosed tribal grandmother, than along the delicate lines of her Malayali mother. The males of her world, all MCPs, looked at her breasts and her thighs and calves and stared twice. But when they raised their eyes to her face, a twist of dismay showed through and they turned and fled. Earlier, when Jenny was young and hopeful, the crude desire followed by quick rejection, hit her hard and she bled inwardly for days. But soon she developed the emotional armour to deflect the blows; over the years the armor thickened into a second skin, a hide almost, so that now it was her eyes that radiated disgust and sent strong men whimpering for cover.

It took Jenny a couple of years to come close to me. Slowly the fact dawned on her that my eyes never shifted away from face, nor did they pulsate with desire for her superb body. I was merely friendly towards her and the friendliness drew her outside herself ever so slowly. Over time but not too slowly my comradeliness changed to passion, and one day she responded, suddenly and gloriously, like a little boy drawn into the street by a summer thundershower.

For a long time, we never talked of marriage: past experience inhibited both of us from even hinting, by a stray word or an expressive wistfulness, that we should start to think of drifting towards the registrar's office. So, without speaking, we told each other that we should retain, indeed guard, our independence. I did not keep a change of clothes, or even a toothbrush or razor in her flat and her nightgown did not hang on the clothes rack in my bedroom. We carried overnight bags when we spent the night in each other's places. And it was never more than a night at a time. We were both mortally afraid, like a sick man taking pethedine, that two nights in a row would make it an addiction. So we enjoyed each other in short bursts of joy, giving and receiving, and scuttled back into our holes like crabs on the beach. Though we worked in the same office—she was and still is the secretary to the general manager of the *Indian Herald*—we rarely met during the day. Several weeks would go by sometimes with only a smile, a brushing of hands in the corridor, a peck on the cheek. And when we joined again, the sparks flew and clashed and danced and merged with the same intensity and brightness.

In keeping with our unspoken agreement, we had not told each other too much about ourselves. From the first moment it had been decided by communicating through a glance, a smile or a touch, that we should explore each other in the present and not gouge out each other's pasts. All she knew was that I had once been married and had two children whom I had not met for decades. I knew only that her grandfather had been an English soldier and her grandmother, the daughter of a tribal chieftain of the Nilgiri Hills. Her parents had died when she was nineteen and she had some brothers and sisters floating around. I had never met them and did not want to meet them and she wanted things to remain that way.

I shook my head, to docket the past in the back of the filing cabinet in my cerebral cortex, and attacked my breakfast. Jenny was reading the racing section of the newspaper as she forked eggs into her mouth and crunched on the toast. She liked to bet occasionally on the horses, small amounts only and when the long shots came off, I would be treated to dinner in a five-star hotel or given a surprise gift. The last one I got was a two-volume set, exquisitely bound in soft leather, of Kant's *Critique of Pure Reason and Critique of Practical Reason.*

'Jenny?'

'Hunnh?'

'I went off my head half an hour ago.'

'You're mad', she mumbled though a mouthful of breakfast, not looking up from her concentrated study of the track trials of the horses running at the next meet at the Bangalore racecourse.

'That's what I said,' I said.

'Look, buster,' she said with her head still buried in the newspaper. 'I know you used to write a humour column in the newspaper but that doesn't make you funny in the head. You're as sane as Art Buchwald.'

'Jenny. Look at me Jenny. Look......at.......me.'

She looked up and into my eyes.

'Don't tell me you're serious?'

'Yes. I'm in deadly earnest. It happened at seven o' clock. You see before you a confirmed schizophrenic.'

'That means split personality, doesn't it?'

'Actually it means splintered personality, but split personality will do as a working definition.'

She grinned: 'Don't worry, darling. My love is vast enough to envelop two of you; or three or four or four or five.'

I couldn't help smiling. 'I'm serious, I tell you.'

'Darling,' she said, 'Every mad man thinks he is the sanest person alive. Every sane person should be allowed to bay at the moon once in a while. Come on, be a good boy and eat up your breakfast. Isn't it getting late? Good Lord, your coffee has gone stone cold. I'll make a fresh cup for you.' She bustled away.

I could see that she was convinced that I was indulging my wacky sense of humor. It was not the time to press the matter further. I realised too that I wanted to explore my transfigured mind before I talked about it. So I finished my breakfast and dawdled over the fresh cup of coffee as Jenny prepared to leave for work.

'I suppose you won't be able to drop me at the office today?' she asked.

'Would you consider it a grave sin if I didn't?'

'I might. I might not. Depends on whether I get a seat in the bus. If I have to stand, you have sinned and have to do penance this evening. There's a Tamil film I want to see and you have to take me. Your fate depends on the Metro Transport.'

She knows I dislike Tamil movies. She loves them and often cries openly in the theatre when the tear-jerker scenes come on. But I love to be with her, even watching or rather dozing through, a Tamil film and rarely refuse to take her to the cinema. Still, we play this little game so that she does not feel bad about forcing me to do something she thinks I may rather not be doing.

I put my arms around her and kissed her on the mouth. 'Okay, love, seat or no seat, we'll go to the pictures today. Now I have to rush.'

I felt a little unhappy. This was the first I had lied to her, even though it was oblique. I could have dropped her off at the office. But I was overwhelmed by a great need for solitude. I wanted to go the Elliot's Beach, stare at the sea and sort out the jigsaw puzzle inside my cranium.

It was barely past nine when I got out of the house, but the heat struck me like a physical blow, piercing my eyeballs and seemingly melting my brain. Hand cupped over my forehead as a shield, I waited for my eyes to adjust to the glare and then walked to my motorcycle. It was a third-hand bike which I had bought ten years ago, after I won a five thousand rupee jackpot at the horse races, through blind luck. I checked the fuel tank and found it less than half-full. Sufficient unto the day—the evil thereof, I should add. I am an ex-professor of English Literature, don't you know?

The bike started sweetly at the first kick. The boy who cleaned our house, washed clothes and was a part-time general factotum also worked as an apprentice to a motor mechanic, and looking after my bike was his pride and joy.

'But not, apparently, for my buttocks,' I groaned as I realised that the motorcycle had been parked on the street and the seat was sizzling under the June sun. It was like sitting on a hot plate. 'Barbecued balls', I yelled as I started off but by the time I rounded Luz corner and sped past the Kapaleeswarar Temple tank, the searing pain subsided. 'Thank you, Madam, the agony is abated.' That insufferable prig, Thomas Babbington Macaulay, made all the more hateful because I once had to teach his biography as a text in college.

I remember a jingle, a variation on a nursery rhyme, which I had composed about Macaulay's supposedly incestuous relationship with his sisters.

*'Little Macaulay*

*Sat in a valley*

*Stroking his sister's thigh.*

*He put in his ...'*

No, the rest of it is unprintable.

# Chapter 4

*'Forget Paolo Friere. True happiness comes only when there is absolutely no choice.'*

—'The Collected Aphorisms

of the Unknown Punter'

Four hours with my feet in the water at Elliot's Beach did not help. It was too hot. Coherent thought was impossible; I was not able to let whatever thoughts came flowing through my consciousness observe the warp and weft of the schizophrenic's mind. The only reality was the heat; and the sweat dripping steadily off my forehead to my nose, to my lips and down to my chin, to the wet sand below.

I gave up and went to the office. I walked into the reporters' room of the *Indian Herald* to a chorus of 'Hi, Bharat' from half-a-dozen reporters whiling away their time between assignments and an elaborate 'Hail, son of Dushyanta and Shakuntala and father of Bhaarat that is India' from George Kunnackal, the resident comic who slumped on his spine in the chief reporter's chair, his feet on the desk.

'Good news, ladies and gentlemen,' I announced. 'You see before you a man who has attained self-realisation. That calls for a treat. Tiffin and coffee for all. Please place your orders with Manickam, our esteemed attendant, nay, respected colleague who will like Hermes, the swift messenger of the Gods, fly on winged bicycle to Udipi Rama Vilas Hotel and return bearing peacocks tongues and masala dosas and such like Ambrosia. Manickam, for me a masala dosa, two vadais and coffee. Get the orders from the rest.'

With the slow precision of the perennially marginally drunk, Manickam shuffled up to me, took the 500-rupee note I had pulled out of my wallet, did a round of the tables taking orders and ever so slowly drifted out of the room. Two years away from retirement, Manickam had worked as the reporters' room peon since the day he joined the *Herald* more than 40 years ago. He was a small man with deep-set eyes that gleamed dully from somewhere halfway in his skull and his cheeks were so sunken, they seemed to meet in the middle of his face. An alcoholic who needed a glass of arrack every couple of hours, he always exuded a fruity stink that identified him from a hundred yards away.

Manickam was like one of the decades-old ceiling fans in the building. Someone, sometime in the dim past had fitted them up and switched them on, no one knew who or when, and they hung there ever after, spinning away slowly, filthy, eternal and unstoppable. They just revolved; no one even seemed to know where the switches were. Someone, in the same way, had keyed Manickam up 40 years ago and he hadn't stopped or slowed down or speeded up. He was a kind of resident ghost; whenever we went into the reporters' room, at noon or midnight, we would find Manickam there, chewing tobacco, his alcohol-laden breath expelling the odour that we all knew we would miss dreadfully if he were to disappear suddenly.

My work that day did not take long. A couple of phone calls to the police control room and the police station at the Government General Hospital were enough to get my crime stories for the day. The night duty reporter would check once again around ten p.m.

The *Herald* did not go in heavily for crime coverage and only rarely did a police beat story find its way to the front page. Like most other English newspapers in India, the *Herald* was still set in the mould created by its erstwhile British owners and newspapermen who had modelled themselves on the Fleet Street heavies like the *London Times*. Only political news was sensationalised; a simple stabbing rated only a filler. It took a multiple murder—stinking corpses of three men, four women and two children found rotting in a suburban house—to jolt chief sub editors into thinking in terms of grisly photographs, 60 point headlines and juicy intros. Banner coverage of suicides, rapes and gang wars was left to the proles of the Indian newspaper world. The language newspapers did it with a vengeance: blood-red poster-type headlines that came down to a third of the page, onomatopoeic journalese which brought blackly into life the knife ripping through flesh and bone, the moans and shrieks of the victims, gushing blood and the mandatorily maniacal visage of the murderer.

I had therefore to spend only a few minutes on the stories. A paragraph on Krishnaveni (19) who swallowed bug poison because she had failed her high school examination;

two paragraphs on a suicide pact between Murugan (21) and Kannamma (16) who jumped into a well, locked in close embrace, because their parents would not allow them to get married - only to be pulled out, spluttering and choking by Kannamma's uncle and betrothed; and one longish paragraph on two fatally run over by a lorry while they were sleeping on a pavement, mentioning the police were on the lookout for the driver and cleaner of the lorry, both of whom were absconding.

* * *

They were waiting for me when I got back home that day at about half past three, in the humid furnace that was the afternoon, sweaty, kurta sticking to my back. I did not notice them as soon as I entered our flat. I went straight to the bathroom, stripped, stood under the shower for a quarter of an hour and only after that did I feel half-way human. Wearing a fresh dhoti and a vest, I strolled back into the living room and slipped Beethoven's Ninth Symphony into the cassette player. I lay back on the couch and let the divine music flow through my bones and muscles and tendons and veins and arteries.

The ancient ceiling fan, like the one in the office, revolved creakingly, fitfully moving around chunks of hot air, like a bored child playing with building blocks. A drowsy numbness pained my sense and it was then that I recognised the presence of the two entities.

They were part of me and yet outsiders. They were there, behind my eyeballs and inside my head and at the same time I could see them standing in front of me on the living room carpet. Parts of my splintered psyche had coalesced into these two gentlemen, I can't use any other description, though I knew as absolute truth the fact that they were forms of energy, fragments of my mind which had coalesced into personalities as real as you, me and the dog at the lamp-post. Yet, I cannot define what they are; at least not in the strait-jacket that is linear logic and so I will not try.

They were good and bad, pure and evil, sympathetic and cynical, brutal and gentle. The Western educated mind has to stick labels on what it perceives; without names, things do not exist for us. And without thinking, I named them Dr Hekyll and Mr Jyde.

'Who are you?' I asked them anyway. I had already started thinking of them as real people.

They looked at each other. Mr Jyde bowed to Dr Hekyll, who cleared his throat. (I am going to describe their actions as if they were human beings. Otherwise I will never be able to communicate effectively with you.) 'As you have already surmised', he said, 'we are part of you, creations of the explosion that made you a schizophrenic.'

'In other words, a nut case,' said Mr Jyde

'How do you know what I have already surmised?'

'Come, come, Bharat,' said Mr Jyde, 'next you will be asking us how we know your name. You know that we are part of you and yet different from you. You will understand as we get better acquainted.'

'Okay,' 'I said. 'Tell me what has happened to me.'

'Think it out for yourself and you will find answers,' said Dr Hekyll. 'Cast your mind back to your vast reading and you will find pointers there.'

I thought. Schizophrenia. A distant memory knocked tentatively at the back door of my skull. I had read something somewhere, about something called a double-bind which causes splitting of the psyche. A little door clicked open and the memory crept in.

Fritjof Capra and his book *'Uncommon Wisdom'*. A conversation with R.D. Laing on Gregory Bateson's theories on psychiatry. I got up and shuffled to the four shelves in which my little library rested. I took out the book and leafed through it until I came to the passage. I read it aloud.

'He (Laing) introduced me to Bateson's double bind theory of schizophrenia which, he told me, had greatly influenced his own thinking. According to Bateson, the double-bind situation is the central characteristic in the communication patterns of families of diagnosed schizophrenics. The behavior labeled as schizophrenic, Laing explained, represents the person's strategy for living in what he has come to experience as an unlivable situation, a situation in which he cannot move, or make a move without feeling pushed and pulled, both from within himself and from the people around him, a situation in which he cannot win, no matter what he does. For example, the double-bind may be set up for a child by contradictory verbal and non-verbal messages, either from one or both parents, with both kinds of messages implying punishment or threats to the child's emotional security. When these situations occur frequently, Laing explained, the double-bind structure may become a habitual expectation in the child's mental life and may generate schizophrenic experiences and behavior.'

I put the book back on the shelf and flopped into my rocking chair. The music system, my only concession to luxury, was now playing The Moonlight Sonata, cold, pure, mathematical.

'And what do you think of the double bind, Mr Bharat Sharma?' asked Dr Hekyll who materialised behind my left eye. I looked inward and saw Mr Jyde too, standing with his arms folded behind his back.

'Wait, Bharat,' said Mr Jyde. 'Let us first see what the good doctor thinks about it.'

'Yes, Dr Hekyll', I said, 'Please enlighten us.'

Dr Hekyll shoved his thumbs into the pockets of his waistcoat and declaimed. 'As your acute minds would have already indicated to you, Mr Bharat Sharma and Mr Jyde, the double-bind is exemplified by the story of the donkey between two equidistant haystacks.'

Mr Jyde: 'Yeah, I've also heard the joke about two donkeys discussing '*Gone with the Wind*'. The first one liked the film but the second thought the book tasted better.'

Dr Hekyll: 'What has that asinine joke got to do with haystacks?'

Mr Jyde: 'I don't know. What has anything got to do with anything? The thought crossed my mind and I expressed it. Don't we live in a free society?'

Dr Hekyll: 'In India, words are free but thoughts are imprisoned in a five thousand year old stasis. Otherwise, why should one billion people be prepared to murder their neighbours over the site of a mosque or a temple?'

Mr Jyde: 'Oh, I don't know. A bit of blood and gore never did a nation much harm. And it keeps them from anti-social activities like cleaning up the streets and teaching their children to be honest.'

I decided to interrupt. These guys were behaving like loonies. 'Gentlemen, gentlemen, Honorable members of the Lok Sabha. Please stick to the subject under discussion. Otherwise, I shall be forced to adjourn the House. Where were you, Dr Hekyll?'

Dr Hekyll: 'I was, before I was rudely interrupted by the Leader of the Opposition, attempting to bring to your kind notice, Mr Speaker, the relationship between the double-bind theory and the story of the donkey between two haystacks. The donkey was unable to decide which haystack he should gorge himself on first. They were equidistant from him, you see. And so he stood rooted there, pinned into immobility by indecision by the double bind. He became catatonic and starved to death.'

Mr Jyde: 'Why didn't the Good Samaritan come along and remove one of the haystacks?'

Dr Hekyll: 'This happened in the year 22 BC in Guduvancheri, which is more than three thousand miles from Samaria. By the time the Good Samaritan got there, the donkey had been dead for five years.'

Dr Jyde: 'Thank you, Doctor, for your enlightening answer. I, too, know the story of the donkey and the haystacks. Two buffaloes, called Dr Hekyll and Mr Jyde, ate up the haystacks and the dead donkey was used in 1977 as the model for a famous statue of the triumph of democracy entitled Free to Freeze or The Gum-Coated Ballot Paper.'

Dr Hekyll: 'If the Honorable Gentleman of the Opposition continues this filibustering, I shall walk out of the House.'

Mr Jyde: 'My apologies. But I plead justification. The Honorable Member adorning the Treasury benches lays himself open to heckling. Ha, ha, ha. I too have become a punster like you, Mr Speaker.'

Dr Hekyll: 'Sir, Mr Speaker, Sir. I seek your protection.'

I donned the serious mien of the presiding officer of a house of Parliament: 'And you shall have it, Dr Hekyll. Please continue. And you, Mr Jyde, if you continue with your infantile behavior in this august House, I shall be forced to name you.'

Dr Hekyll: 'The tale of the donkey and the haystacks lies at the heart of the double bind: two choices, two conflicting pressures. Man cannot choose. He is free to choose but not free to exercise his freedom. There is either an implosion: catatonia; or an explosion: a splitting schizophrenia or multiple personalities. QED.'

Mr Jyde: 'That, as my eighth class maths teacher said, stands for Quite Easily Done.'

Dr Hekyll: 'Pshaw!'

He walked off in a huff into the basement of my brain.

Mr Jyde: 'He gets bugged so easily, doesn't he, Bharat? And how shall we enjoy the rest of the day, my friend, till your good wife gets back? Any juicy thoughts of murder, rape and mayhem? Shall we start a communal riot? Throw dead pigs into a mosque or kill the fatted calf in the temple? Or shall we only indulge a little, a spot of defloration maybe? I espy two virgins, ripe for rape, titillating tits jiggling down the street. Or is it going to be a spark of arson? Shall we set fire to the Reichstag?'

# Chapter 5

*'The child's father is the father of the man'*
—'The Collected Aphorisms of the Unknown Punter'

Once again it happened when I least expected it. I had finished typing a news report and was about to hit the transmit key when my hand froze; or so I was told by my colleagues in the reporters' room. And, strangely, they said the stasis lasted for less than a minute though the conversation I had with Mr Jyde surely lasted an hour at least. How was that? One more of those questions that should not be asked?

I was not aware of anything outside my inner space.

'Are you there, Dr Hekyll?' I called.

'No, he isn't,' answered Mr Jyde. 'He has gone to Manasarovar to meditate on the eternal verities expounded by Robert Louis Stevenson with whom, as you must be aware, he was rather well acquainted in one of his previous avatars as Dr Jekyll. But I am at your disposal, as always, Bharat. I do not need to meditate on Stevenson for I occupied, for some time, the mind of Robert Louis.'

'Thank you, Mr Jyde. I was thinking about that bit we read on the contradictory verbal and non-verbal messages a child gets. Have you any further thoughts on that?'

'My dear Bharat I have, for your sake, been thinking of little else.'

'Have you formed any conclusions?'

'Conclusions? No, not anything firm,' said Mr Jyde. 'But let us look at the proposition, not syllogistically but elliptically, in the form of a parable.'

'Sure, I love stories.'

'Picture this,' Mr Jyde said.

A middle class residence in any city or large town in India. Probably a third floor flat in a building which does not have an elevator. Two tiny bedrooms, a small drawing-dining. It is late evening. The mother is in the kitchen, cooking dinner. The father is on the sofa-cum-bed, reading a film gossip magazine. The daughter, who has just entered college, is studying at her tiny table in the second bedroom. The son, about 13 years old, is dribbling a football in the drawing-dining, kicking it under the dining table and then dangerously close to the colour TV set on which 24 instalments still have to be paid.

The father throws away the film magazine with a snort of prurient disgust. The football whizzes past his ear, slams off the wall, bounces of the edge of the TV set and hits him on the nose.

Eyes streaming with tears of pain, the father shouts: 'Stop that, you little bastard.'

'Don't use bad language dear.' A faint whine from the kitchen.

'Sorry,' shouts the father at the kitchen wall. He grabs his son's shoulder and twists his ear.

'How many times have I told you not to play football inside the house?'

The pugnaciously silent son thinks: 'He didn't say anything about my kicking the ball around for the past half hour when he was reading that rubbishy film magazine.'

The father, in a less loud voice: 'Why do you do it? Why do you play football in the house when I have forbidden you to do it?'

'I was bored'

'Children should not be bored. There are a hundred thousand things you could and should be doing.'

'Name two.'

'Well, you could ... Well, you should ....Don't be bloody impertinent.'

'Didn't mother tell you not to use bad words?'

The father controls himself with an effort. 'Bloody is okay when adults use it. It is a bad word for children.'

The father tries to make up for his bad temper. 'So, you're bored, are you? Come, I will tell you a story.'

The boy's face lights up with joy and excitement. 'He Man? Star Wars? Not Aladdin and the Wonderful Lamp again, please?'

The father sits down on the sofa-cum-bed. 'No, no, none of those. Come sit next to me and I will tell you a story that my father told me when I was your age.'

'Once upon a time, there was a father and a son, just like you and me. They lived in a village near a forest. The boy was very timid. The other children in the village had lots of fun climbing trees and jumping off the branches. But this boy never joined them. He was afraid. One day, his father took him to the edge of the forest and told him to climb the lowermost branch of a tree which was about ten feet above the ground.'

'The boy demurred, shrinking away. The father gave him a pep talk. 'Why do you worry when I am here? You won't be hurt. I'll look after you. Come on, be a brave lad and climb on to that branch.'

'The boy hesitated. He moved towards the tree and moved away, went near the tree and scrambled back. The father encouraged him again and the boy finally screwed up enough courage to climb the tree. He sat fearfully on the lowest branch, legs dangling and hands gripping the wood so tightly that his arms started aching.'

''Now jump,' said the father. The boy shook his head violently. 'No, no, no,' he shouted. The father once again encouraged the boy to jump. 'Why should you worry when I am here? I am your father. I will not let you get hurt. Jump and I will catch you.'

'The boy believed his father. He closed his eyes and slid off the branch. He fell on the ground in a heap. His father had not moved an inch to catch him.'

'The boy was not hurt at all. Just a few bruises. But he started crying, sobbing as if his heart were broken. 'Why didn't you catch me? Why didn't you catch me? Why didn't you catch me?' he kept asking his father.'

'The father picked up the boy, held him in his arms and soothed him.' Son, he said, 'I wanted to teach you two things. One, you shouldn't be afraid of climbing trees. Two, never trust anybody. Not even your father. Always question what somebody says. That way, you'll never get hurt''.

In the little flat, the father places him on the sofa-cum-bed. 'Did you like that story?'

'No,' cries the son. 'What a horrible father that was. How can he say that a son should not trust his father?'

'Son,' says the father, 'the story is not about trusting people. The moral is never take anything at face value. Always ask questions. Anyway, this story is hundreds of years old and therefore its moral should have some validity.'

Mr Jyde continued:

Half an hour later. The father is reading the film magazine and the son is sprawled on the floor, drawing crude pictures of his comic strip heroes.

'Son, what do you want to be when you grow up?'

'A fighter pilot.'

(I butted in. 'He should become a commercial pilot. Then he has a chance of becoming the Prime Minister of India.'

Mr Jyde: 'Hah, hah. Good one, Bharat. Now, will you please let me get on with enlightening you?')

The father asks: Why not an engineer like me? Or a doctor? Or a scientist?'

The son thinks about this. 'Yeah, why not? Any one of them. But a doctor would be best. Doctors make tons of money. My classmate's father is a doctor and he comes to school every day in a Hyundai car. Not like me. I get crushed in the school bus every day.'

The father is shaken, but doesn't show it. His salary is not high. He is just able to save a little through insurance policies. He composes himself and says: 'Son, whatever you want to do, decide once and for all and stick to your decision. Don't be a rolling stone.'

Son: 'Why shouldn't I be a rolling stone?'

Father: 'Because a rolling stone gathers no moss.'

Son: 'Why should a stone gather moss?'

Father: 'Now you are being impertinent. I don't like sarky children. I don't want to hear anything more about this.'

Son: 'But why should it, Daddy? Why should a stone gather moss?'

Father: 'You want me to take out my belt? Then don't question what your elders tell you.'

Son: 'But Daddy, you told me half an hour ago that I should question everything that ...'

He is interrupted by a roar of anger. 'Shut up.' The father begins to unbuckle his belt.

Son, shrinking back against the wall, hands raised in feeble protection: 'I'm sorry, Daddy. I'm sorry.'

The father subsides. Silence, for about ten minutes.

'Daddy?'

'Unhnh?'

'Daddy, I still don't understand.'

'What don't you understand, my little pet?

'I don't understand why it should be an essential quality of a stone that it gathers moss.'

'What's that?'

'Why should a stone gather moss, Daddy?'

'There you go again, you bloody brat.'

Whack. Whack. Whack.

The next day. In school. The English class. The teacher: 'So that is how Mowgli was saved by his animal friends from the fury of the ferocious tiger Shere Khan. Any questions?'

The boy: 'Sir, was Mowgli a rolling stone?'

Teacher: 'What's that?'

Boy: 'Mowgli kept moving from place to place in the forest. That makes him a rolling stone, doesn't it? My father says you should not be a rolling stone.'

Teacher: 'Your father is correct. A rolling stone gathers no moss.'

Boy: 'But why should a rolling stone gather moss, Sir? Why can't it keep on rolling, with no moss to slow it down?'

Teacher: 'It is a proverb. Proverbs are never wrong. They are the essence of ancient wisdom. You should never question a proverb.'

Boy (thinks): 'You shouldn't trust your father but a proverb will never fail you.'

Teacher: 'Here's another proverb. Neither a borrower nor a lender be.'

Boy (thinks): 'That's not a proverb. It's Polonius advising his son Laertes in Shakespeare's Hamlet. But if I tell the teacher that, he will make me stand up on the bench.'

But the boy cannot suppress his inquisitive spirit: 'Sir, please Sir.'

'Yes, my boy.'

'Sir, if everybody follows the proverb and is neither a lender nor a borrower, how can there be any banks and how will my father get a loan from his office to buy a scooter?'

'You want to stand up on the bench?'

'No, Sir.'

'They don't ask impertinent questions. Learn to respect your elders. Don't contradict what they say. Little boys should be seen, not heard. Any other questions?'

'Of course not, Sir.'

'Then, class dismissed.'

'I suppose the kid grew up to be a schizo like me?' I asked Mr Jyde.

'No', he said, chuckling. 'He was lucky. The spirit of inquiry flowering in him was killed by the droughts of what parent, teacher, priest and nurse taught. But his natural creative urges turned to art. He became a painter; not a great one but good enough to become rich. He migrated to the United States.'

'I suppose a lot of rich Americans bought his paintings?'

My Jyde laughed: 'He didn't sell a single painting. Even sleazy restaurants, Indian, Chinese, Italian, Puerto Rican, refused to take them. Even as gifts. After trying his hand for some years as a painter, he joined an advertising agency, drawing illustrations for ads. He worked his way up, creating brilliant bits of nonsense for highly successful ads which really managed to sell things. Now, he heads a largish agency on Madison Avenue. He has his own brownstone in New York, a country house, three cars, a yacht, two Poodles and a Pekinese.'

'Is this story true, Mr Jyde?'

'Does it matter?'

'No, I suppose not. I just wondered.'

'It's true all right.'

'How do you know? Did you hear it from someone?'

'My dear Bharat,' said Mr Jyde, patting my limbic system gently, as if he were fondling a pet cat, 'I am not just a splinter of your mind, a mere creation of the fission of your psyche. I am also a bit of Atman which again is a shard of omnipresent Brahman. So is Dr Hekyll. So are you. So are millions of others like us. We are eternal and have lived, together or separately, in billions of souls and minds since our existence began with the ripples that shook omniscient Brahman after the first big boom of Om. We usually reside deep under the conscious mind, unknown to the individual. Sometimes, as when we are injected into interesting minds like yours, we surface and enjoy the pleasures of intellectual discourse and emotional companionship. I was in that boy's brain for a few years when he started his advertising career. That is how I know the story is true.'

'What about me?' I asked. 'Do you think I have become what I am, because of what was done to me in my youth?'

'You tell me.'

'I don't know. I can only describe. I cannot deduce.'

'Description is one way of arriving at the truth. The western linear process of thinking often leads to absurd conclusions, which are logically unshakeable.'

'How's that?' I asked.

Mr Jyde grinned, 'Take the famous syllogism.

All men die.

Socrates is a man.

Therefore, Socrates must die.

Now, consider this,' Mr Jyde continued.

'Socrates must die.

All pigs die.

Therefore, Socrates is a pig.

See what I mean? See where linear thinking can get you if you are not careful?'

I thought circularly for a while. 'You know', I said, 'Socrates really was a pig. I have read that he wore filthy clothes and rarely had a bath.'

'Bravo, Bharat. Now you are learning to think properly.'

# Chapter 6

*'One man's nightmare is another man's wet dream'*

—Philip Hose Farmer

Mr Jyde started saying something, but Dr Hekyll elbowed him aside and took centre stage, at the mid-point between my eyebrows. He stuck his hands into his waistcoat pockets and declaimed:

*'The time has come, the walrus said,*

*To talk of many things;*

*Of ships, of shoes, of sealing wax,*

*Of cabbages and kings.*

*Of why the sea is boiling hot,*

*And whether pigs have wings.*

*And, of course, why our friend*

*Is in his own nut-house.'*

Mr Jyde pushed Dr Hekyll aside and took his place. 'Those last two lines are terrible, aren't they, Bharat? And now, 'Absent thee from felicity awhile and tell thy story.'

And thus I began to tell the story of the most important part of my life, a series of events that pushed me off into a tangent of misery.

I passed the MA English Literature exam with a first class and first rank in the University. I was immediately offered a job as a lecturer in English in the Presidency College from which I graduated. My father died when I was still an undergraduate and I finished my education on scholarships and a bank loan. My mother died soon after. Life was tough but I was happy. I love the English language. I see the language as a guru, a friend, a mistress, a wife and a beloved child who grows and changes and delights every day. I tried, in my lectures, to pass on to my students this deep emotional attachment to the language, this feeling of awe and love, rather than to merely explain to them the meaning and nuances of the texts and prepare them to pass the examinations, to get degrees and to land jobs.

I also started working on my doctorate, 'Humour and wit in English Literature from Dryden to P. G. Wodehouse.' That was a fascinating journey. God, those fellows knew how to make you laugh and wither inside as if you were the object of their surgical sarcasm.

I was happy. Each year, my class was the usual mixed bag. Many of my students had been fed on a low-calorie intellectual diet and were there only because they could not get in anywhere else, but some were there because they liked to study English Literature. I was a keen cricketer—opening bat and leg spinner. I had captained the college in my final year and continued to play first division league cricket. I played a couple of Ranji trophy matches too. After getting my doctorate in two years, I started working on a book which I wanted to call 'The Proper Study: A critique of English Humour', an expanded version of my doctoral thesis. My days were full, free and glorious; my life eudemonistic. Up at six, a few exercises and some jogging on the spot, shit-shave-shower, prepare for the day's lectures till nine, breakfast, and off to college. In the evening, cricket at the nets with the college team, back home by seven, work on my book till eleven and off to bed. My holidays were spent in the Connemara Library and swimming in the sea off Elliot's Beach. As I said before, I led a full, free and glorious life.

I did not smoke or drink then. I could not afford to and I did not need to. The great change came when I met her. She was my student in the MA class. As the current coinage then had it, the heartthrob of every male student; or as the current coinage now has it, the all-time-great prick-teaser.

A beauty she was—Renuka Kailasam—and still is. Long black hair flowing down to below her buttocks, heart-shaped face, 'wheat-complexioned' as they say in the matrimonial ads, great, almond-shaped eyes that seemed to swim mistily, full lips that promised to suck forth your soul, breasts that were big without being heavy, a body that was lush without being coarse, slim waist flowing out into wide hips tapering down to trim calves and exquisite feet. She would have been the greatest sex-goddess of Indian films had she gone to Bombay.

There she was, every day, in the front row of the class, breasts pillowed on crossed arms as she leaned forward intently, apparently unwilling to miss a single word I uttered. I thought it was my 'brilliant' lectures that enraptured her but she was out to get me from the first day. 'It was love at first sight for me, darling,' she told me once. Later, I realised that she had been husband-hunting since she was sixteen. She found what she sought in me—meek, modest, and brilliant in a line that had, for her little practical use, a showpiece and an object she could dominate without fear of rebellion. Maybe she did love me a little. I am not sure and after all these years I don't think I really care whether she did or did not. She is one of the strongest personalities I have met and I was then a weak one, that's not to say I am very strong now. She trapped me within three months of the day she entered my class.

Renuka was the sole heir to a family of bankers. Her father was the chairman of a flourishing bank in Madras, which had been started by his grandfather. His dream and Renu's was to make her the first woman chief executive of a bank in India. She had studied commerce in Miranda House in Delhi (no Madras college was good enough for her) and then went on to the Delhi School of Economics. She was quite brilliant academically. Her purpose in moving to English Literature was part of her long-term strategy, which included a stint at the Harvard Business School—she went there after we separated. She wanted to polish the granite of her mind and soul. English literature would give her an outward intellectual softness which would camouflage the hard businesswoman inside. Imagine a lady banker quoting Keats and Eliot at a cocktail party—her clients and competitors would dismiss her as an heiress with business ambitions but addled by romantic nonsense, and look away while she slammed them in the crotch.

She wanted a husband who would be her opposite in every way, a dull background to provide the contrast. And she wanted a high-class sperm bank to fill her with seed; but not too many of those either. She was, and still is, the sexiest woman I have met but was curiously sexless;

agamic almost. Her sexual drive was abnormally low. To her, sex was useless if its only purpose was an orgasm. To put it in bankers' terms, the spending had to be balanced with some income.

She did nothing for the first month, except to overwhelm me with her apparent fascination for my lectures and the sincerity of her efforts to master English Literature. She had a first-rate mind; her questions in class were the most pertinent, sometimes emitting a flash of brilliance that illuminated a whole lecture hour. I soon thought of her as the best student I had had the pleasure to teach. All the other men in the college, the principal included, considered her the best prospective lay they had come across.

One day, I did not cycle to college. I was to talk that evening to a discussion group formed by students in Adyar, on the effects of the two world wars on English poetry, and it was too far away to cycle in comfort. Renu made her first move that evening.

After classes, which ended at four, I strolled across to the Marina Buhari restaurant for a cup of tea. I had time to kill, for the meeting was set for six. After dawdling over the tea, I walked slowly to the bus stop opposite the Marina cricket ground. I intended to get off at Sathya Studios and walk across the Adyar Bridge to Gandhinagar. As I crossed the Kannagi statue and neared the bus stop, a car screeched to a halt near me and I heard Renuka ask: 'Sir, may I give you a lift?'

'Thank you, Miss Kailasam, but no. You see, I am not going to my house in Mylapore. I am going to Adyar.'

'That's no problem. I am going to Adyar too, to call on a friend. Hop in and I'll drop you. Please?'

She was leaning across the front seat to look up at me through the window, as I leaned in. Her sari had slipped to her waist. My eyes kept darting between her face and the deep cleavage exposed by her low-cut blouse. At the word 'please', I lifted my face and looked into her eyes. That was the moment which put my soul into reverse gear.

I opened the door and dropped like a sack of potatoes on the front seat. Renu took off quickly, keeping the car in third gear as she overtook three buses and a lorry. She drove very fast but was confident, switching in and out of the traffic with a light touch on the steering wheel. I was nervous and my throat was dry. Passing the Gandhi statue, she slowed down to a more comfortable speed.

'Please don't think I drive like a maniac all the time, Sir. It's just that I feel nervous and restless today. I don't know why.' She looked at me and smiled.

'Miss Kailasam', I said, 'I am sure that you are really a safe and responsible driver.'

'Sir, why do you keep calling me Miss Kailasam? I am your student and you have every right to call me Renuka. In fact, it would make me very happy if you called me Renu, as my friends do. You are my friend, aren't you?' She looked at me again and smiled and blushed faintly.

I was startled. Only the previous week I had heard her savagely snub a classmate who called her Miss Renuka. 'The name, Mr Santhanakrishnan, is Miss Kailasam.' The frigid haughtiness made me happy I was not at the receiving end. The poor fellow had shrunk into his shirt, muttered something and slunk away, probably wishing the earth would open up and swallow him.

'Well...er...that's fine Miss...I mean Renuka...of course, friends… I mean Renu...but...' I was incapable of stringing four words together.

'But what will the college say? It will be between us. In college we will be models of perfect student-teacher behavior. But outside...' She left the sentence hanging, as she swiftly overtook a bus, poaching well into the wrong side of the road and avoiding an oncoming truck by a whisker, with a sharp swerve to the left.

'That was close, Sir. Were you frightened?'

'No, I was not...Yes, I was petrified.' We laughed immoderately.

She insisted on attending the discussion. 'It's a fascinating subject, Sir. How selfish of you not to tell me. I must attend. I must listen to you. Do take me, Sir, I'm sure they won't mind.'

After the lecture, I slipped into the front seat of her car as if it was the most natural thing to do. Halfway to my house, she turned to me and asked 'Where do you usually have dinner?'

'Oh, I generally cook something for myself. I can make a passable sambar and an edible potato curry, but that's the limit. I manage somehow.'

'But what about tonight? It's already half past eight. What will you do? It will be ten by the time you finish cooking and you'll be so hungry.'

'I'll manage somehow, Renu.' It had become surprisingly natural to call her Renu. 'If I don't feel like cooking, there is always the Udipi restaurant at Luz Corner.'

She was silent for a few minutes. We arrived at my house. She switched off the engine and turned to me, shyly: 'Sir, I know it's impertinent and perhaps you'll get angry, but I don't care. Would you mind having dinner with me?' She lowered her head and then looked up, flashing a quick smile before becoming serious again.

I pondered for a moment, but only a moment. Perhaps a thought about the proper student-teacher relationship feebly nudged the outer layer of my subconscious, but it soon sank far below the surface. I wanted to be with the girl, look at her, hear her talk, see her move her hands, her head, walk with her. For the first time in my life, I just wanted to be with a woman.

'Okay, Renu. Tonight, I shall stuff myself with gastronomical and ocular delights.'

She threw me a dazzling smile which left me weak and made my thighs turn to water. 'Where shall we go? Do you eat non-vegetarian food?'

'I've tried chicken a couple of times and liked it.'

'Lovely, we'll go to the Club. The Coronation Club, I'm a member.'

Though it should be one of my most vivid memories, I don't remember much of that dinner, except that we dined on the lawns of the club and that neither of us spoke much.

It was nearing eleven when she dropped me home. 'Won't your parents be worried?' I asked.

'No Sir they won't, as long as I am home by eleven.'

I got out of the car and leaned in through the window.

She shifted on the seat, turning towards me. 'Good night, Sir.' She put out her hand. I took it in mine. It was deliciously soft and the touch set up a tingling in me.

'Renu.' My voice was hoarse. 'You are being unfair. I call you Renu but you keeping calling me Sir. Why don't you call me Bharat?'

'No. I won't. I can't. At least, not till...'

'Till when, Renu?'

'She said nothing; simply squeezed my hand; slid back behind the wheel and drove off quickly without another word.

We were married three months later.

* * *

There was no proposal, from either side. Within a few days of that dinner we came to a tacit decision that we would get married as soon as possible. No words were necessary. One day she did not come to class and that evening she came home, a little tearful, but triumphant. Her father had agreed to our getting married and wanted to see me the next evening. Her father had kicked up a big row at first, she told me. He had roared and ranted about the dreams he had for his only child and here she was, throwing herself and her family pride, honour and inheritance away on a worthless, Brahmin school-teacher—he never called me anything other than school-teacher or son-in-law, depending on his mood. But she had been adamant, she told me. 'Our love held me firm, Bharat. Each time I felt myself wavering, your beloved face floated across my mind's eye and I was strong again.' Yechh, what gunk and goo. But at that time it was nectar to my ears, I was so far gone.

I pulled her close and kissed her hand, her lips, bit her neck and nuzzled between her breasts. 'You're wonderful', I breathed.

Once she got her breath back, she said: 'I used some powerful arguments. He wants to meet you tomorrow, around seven in the evening, at our house.'

'Do I have to wear a suit or something?' I was already becoming tense.

She calmed me by running her fingers lightly through my hair and chastely kissing me on the cheek. 'Of course not, darling. Don't be nervous. He's not going to eat you.'

The early part of the next day was not the torture I had imagined it would be. I had a full lecture schedule and a tonne of assignments to mark. But, as the day wore on, the tension started building up. To work it off, I bowled at the nets for over an hour. I got home only around six. Renu was waiting for me. 'Hurry up, darling. We don't want to be late.'

'There's plenty of time, darling. A quick shower and change of clothes will find me ready to face my destiny... Or rather, the man of my destiny.' The last bit was muttered under my breath. I knew I was not going to like my prospective father-in-law.

The evening was worse than the worst nightmare. The man simply bulldozed me, battered my ego, crushed my character and left me a glob of senseless flesh, quivering on the exquisite Persian carpet in his drawing room.

He was courteous for the first thirty seconds after we were introduced. He shook my hand, patted my back and guided me to a sofa so deep and yielding that, when I sat, my knees were almost level with my chin. I had to struggle hard to get to my feet. It was his first dirty trick. And then there was that expression on his face as he towered over me. His face seemed to say: 'Is this the shit I'm getting for a son-in-law? It's all karma I suppose, for the sins I committed in my previous life.'

'Well, Mr Sharma...'

'In fact, it is Dr Sharma.'

'What?'

'I mean the proper form of address is Dr Sharma. I have a doctorate in English Literature. The subject of my thesis was 'Humour and Wit in English Literature from Dryden to P G Wodehouse.'

I must have been incrediblye tense and nervous to babble such nonsense.

I could see the effect it was having on Kailasam. His face was even more expressive, broadcasting his thoughts: 'My God, I don't believe it. I knew it would be bad; but such rubbish? My karma couldn't be so bad!'

'Well, 'Doctor' Sharma, my daughter says you want to marry her. What have you to offer her?'

'Nothing but myself, my love and my intellect.'

I know I couldn't have been such a pompous ass, but I swear I was. I can never forget a single word of what was said that evening.

'I hear that you have already giving her something from another part of your body.'

'Mr Kailasam, I do not understand what you mean.'

'Doctor Sharma', the big man snarled, concentrating in his vocal chords the fury that filled his six-foot two-inch frame. 'Doctor Sharma, you were supposed to fill my daughter's head with English prose, poetry, fiction and drama. But you have pumped her belly full of something else. I suppose you acted on the principle that the best way to a man's heart, and to his money, is through his daughter's stomach via her vagina.'

I was bewildered at first, and then furious. I struggled to get out that damned sofa and on to my feet to drive my first into Kailasam's filthy mouth. My eyes fell on Renu who was standing behind and to the left of her father. There was a pleading look on her face, her finger covered her lips in a mute appeal to me to keep quiet, and made shushing motions with her other hand. She was dressed in one of those north-Indian salwar-kameez things, which clung to her prick-raising body, more closely than I wanted to cling to it. A thrill passed through me, fury transmuted into desire, as realisation came of what she had done. So this was one of the powerful arguments she had used.

She had lied to her father that she was pregnant by me and that marriage was the only way out; in those days abortion was a greater crime than fornication. And then I wanted to laugh, let go completely, roll about clutching my stomach on the sofa and the Persian carpet. I took a deep breath, and clasped my hands tightly to control the rising hysteria and sank back, knees once again at chin level. I thought of Renu sprawled naked on my marriage bed and swore I would take revenge.

'Sir', it came out as a croak and I cleared my throat. 'Well Sir', I still sounded like a crow but to hell with it. 'I can only plead that such things happen because of the folly of young love and that you must be magnanimous.'

Kailasam switched his mood to grudging consent. 'What's done is done I suppose and can't be undone. I formally give my consent to your marriage with my daughter.'

Renu sprang into action. She chattered brightly: 'I'll go and make some coffee. You two get to know each other. And behave yourselves, both of you.' She practically ran out of the room.

I felt I had to get a bit of my own back.

'Sir,' I said stiffly, 'I think it was unnecessary for you to use the words 'and his money' when talking about the way to a man's heart.'

Kailasam was a trained conversational heavyweight. He swatted aside my roundhouse swing and ripped off a short left hook to the jaw. 'Of course, it was unnecessary. It is always unnecessary to state the obvious.'

Call the referee and stop the bout!

Kailasam pulled out a gold cigarette case. 'Don't smoke, I suppose?' His eyes translated the words into 'milksop', the son of a bitch.

I stared back defiantly. Of course I did not smoke.

'I'd like one.' I said. I did not move to take a cigarette from the case he offered me, still staring blindly at him. I couldn't have stood up anyway without an undignified wrestling match with the sofa's deep springs and swan's-down cushions. He got up and came across to me. I took a cigarette and he lit it with a flick of his gold Ronson lighter. I took a puff and felt I was going to explode.

'Drink?'

I nodded, unable to speak, desperately trying not to cough my guts out.

'Scotch and soda?'

I nodded again. He walked over to the liquor cabinet and started mixing the drinks. 'Renu', he shouted, 'No need for coffee. We're having something stronger.'

The interruption gave me a respite. With a supreme effort of will, I let the smoke gush out without coughing and took a deep breath. He came back with the glasses, handed me one and went back to his chair. I gulped and almost gagged. The bloody thing was like fire, burning my throat and oesophagus, settling like a live coal in my stomach. The bastard had filled half the glass with whisky, the rest with ice and added a mere splash of soda. My eyes started watering.

'Yes', he said, grinning venomously, 'It is a happy occasion. But I always thought it was the bride and the mother who cried.'

Once again he switched the line of attack. Now it was soft-sell. 'Son, you don't have to impress me. I know you don't smoke and drink. I can tell by the way you handle your cigarette and your glass. (I later found out that he had had me investigated by a private detective agency). I've agreed to the marriage and I never go back on my word.'

His voice had softened amazingly and his words, his face, his entire body, were those of a benign uncle. I put my cigarette down in the ash tray and my glass on the side table, looking at him with something akin to hope. Maybe he had behaved so badly because of the shock of learning that his daughter had a bastard in her womb; maybe he would turn out to be a nice chap after all.

But the man was a master psychologist. The avuncular switch had further softened me for the kill, but the knife to the jugular was still to come. Now he became a fairy godmother showering gifts.

'Certain practical matters have to be settled.'

Renu walked into the room. Her eyebrows almost hit her hairline when she saw the smoldering cigarette and drink near me.

Kailasam turned to Renu. 'I told him he need not try to impress me. He has impressed me enough. Now, Renu, leave us alone for ten minutes. This is man talk.'

She blushed prettily, already the bride, and head bowed slowly floated out of the room. The performance alone should have won her a medal from the Delhi University Dramatic Society.

'Now Doctor Sharma.' No more of that vile stress on the word 'doctor.' 'Bharat?...Okay, Bharat. Now, Bharat, since both your parents are dead and you have no close elderly relatives, I have taken upon myself the job of making some decisions about how this marriage is to take place. I am sure you don't mind and I hope you will concur with what I have decided.'

He did not wait for me to express my concurrence. 'The marriage will be a simple affair, not more than 200 guests. A registered marriage with a short homam, I'd like that. It will give a touch of culture, but no elaborate rituals. You would prefer it like that I suppose?'

'Yes, Sir. I'm not particularly religious and have none to please in that respect.'

'That's settled then. The marriage will be on the twentieth of November, a week from now. I'll host a reception that evening to which I will probably invite the whole of Madras. Okay with you?'

'The sooner, the better.'

Now a touch of steel crept into his tone. 'The dowry… no, no, young man, I will not allow you to interrupt. My daughter's dowry is a matter of the greatest prestige for me and my family.'

He paused, letting me soak in his pride and his generosity.

'The dowry will be: ten lakh rupees in a five-year fixed deposit in your name, solely in your name, in my bank. A five-bedroom house in Wallace Garden, Nungambakkam, fully furnished. And by fully furnished, I mean fully, from the doorbell to the potato peeler: the furnishings to be chosen by Renu. Plus, a car for you and one for her. On the day the first child is born, 20 lakh rupees will be put in a trust fund with three of us as trustees. When the child reaches the age of 21, the money will pass to him, but only if all the three trustees agree that it will not lead to his ruination. If even one of them refuses to sign the release, he will have to wait another five years, when it will become his unconditionally, no permission needed from the trustees. The same rules will hold for every other child born. Agreed?'

'You're...you're most generous, sir.'

'It's my daughter who is getting married. But there is one final condition.'

Before he could state it, Renu came back. She had changed into a demure silk sari. It was a quick change from lover to bride to wife.

'I'm glad you are here, Renu,' Kailasam said, strong and steely. 'I want you to hear this. This is the key condition. If you do not agree to it, I wash my hands of the whole affair. The condition, Bharat, is that you will resign your job in the Presidency College and take up a position in my bank. No son-in-law of mine is going to be a damned schoolteacher.'

I jumped out of the sofa, no struggle this time. This was going too far.

'I'm afraid, sir, the condition is impossible. Teaching English is my life. I won't earn much. I have no qualms of conscience about letting my wife live on her own money. But I must teach. I must, I must. Surely you realise that if I worked in a bank, my intellect and my soul would wither and die. Surely, you can see that. Please don't force me to do this.' I was pleading and even as I did, I knew that by pleading, I had lost.

'No marriage unless you chuck up that shitty job and come into my bank', Kailasam growled. 'Accept that condition and you can marry Renu. Refuse and you can walk out right now. What's more important to you, being married to Renu or your job? Decide; and decide in the next five minutes.' Theatrically, he strode to the French window and stared out, leaving Renu and me facing each other.

Renu put her hands on my shoulders and looked up into my face. I avoided looking into her eyes.

'Bharat, a bank job's not all that bad. You can always write in your free time. I won't make too many demands on you.'

'But I want to teach, not write. Teaching is my gift to the future.'

'Darling, humour him now. A year later he'll cool down and you can go back to teaching. I'm sure he'll relent. I promise you I won't give him a moment's peace till he agrees. But for now, please say yes. Look at me, look into my eyes. Please say you'll do this for me.'

I looked into her eyes. We were married the next week.

# Chapter 7

*'Never, never, never, never, never.'*

—King Lear, Act V, scene V

'Phew, that was cruel,' said Dr Hekyll.

'You really got kicked in the crotch, pal:' Mr Jyde. 'But please continue; you obviously haven't finished this chapter of your life yet.'

We went to Kashmir for our honeymoon, (I continued). The day after we returned, I joined the bank as a Public Relations Officer. Renu and her father told me that this was the best place to start, to prepare for a senior executive position. 'An efficient and effective PRO', Kailasam lectured me, 'has to know a little about what is going on and what is done in every section of the bank. Only then can he maintain good liaisons with the clients. All round knowledge is essential before you can become a senior manager.'

I knocked on the door of the PR department at the stroke of ten. 'Come in', quavered a thin, reedy voice. I walked in, stopped and stared. My heart sank till I thought I could feel it beating somewhere below my left knee.

The PRO's office was two doors away from the fifth floor toilets, separated from the loo by a broom closet, which was not big enough to keep fully at bay the phenyl-drenched stench of stale urine. Neither was the room much bigger than the broom closet, perhaps twelve feet by ten. As you entered, the entire wall on the right was taken up by floor-to-ceiling open wooden shelves, which were stacked with dusty newspapers. There were two desks, both piled about a foot high with files, newspapers and press clipping in folders. Behind the larger desk sat the incumbent PRO, while the other was for the peon who brought in a pile of newspapers every morning and took away the dismembered remains in the evening.

The man behind the chair looked like a clerk about to be superannuated. 'Ah yes, Mr Bharat Sharma. My name is Thothadriraman. I had a memo about you yesterday from the Chairman's Secretary. You are to be trained as a PRO. But before we start, may I offer you my congratulations on your good fortune?'

He propped an elbow on a stack of files in front of him and stuck his hand out, and withdrew it hastily as I kept staring at him.

'I am sorry, it was impertinent of me, an ordinary clerk to offer his best wishes to the husband of the daughter of the Chairman', he said plaintively, drawing himself up with what he thought was dignity.

'No, it is I who should be sorry, Mr Thothadriraman. It was remiss of me. Thank you very much. I was thinking about something else. Please accept my apologies, may I sit down?'

'Of course, of course. Please do. How remiss of me not to ask you to sit down.' Thothadri was all smiles now. He rushed around his table, lifted the peon's chair from behind the second desk, placed it in front of his desk, dusted it with his dhoti and scuttled back to his chair. I sat down and wished I had a cigarette.

'Let us begin at the beginning, Mr Sharma. What are the functions of the PR department? That is exactly the question you would like to ask?'

'Yes, Mr Thothadri, you couldn't have put it better.' But this man was sarcasm-proof.

'What does the PR department do? What every PR department does, I suppose. We arrange press conferences when the Chairman wants them. You know, send out invitations to the newspapers: The Chairman of the bank cordially invites so-and-so to a press conference at such-and-such place at such-and-such time. If it is after 7 p.m., we add cocktails or dinner. If it is in the day, we say tea or lunch. In fact, the invitations come down directly from the Chairman's office. We merely write down the addresses and post the invitations.'

'Most of the press conferences are held in the Chairman's private suite on the tenth floor; we do not have to bother about making arrangements with the hotels. If it is dinner and cocktails, the Chairman decides the menu and the type of drinks; the orders are sent out directly to the caterers. All we have to do is welcome the reporters as they come in. If any of them gets too drunk, the security staff quietly take him out and send him home in a company car.'

It was getting worse by the minute and I tried to cheer myself up by taking it out on poor Thothadri. 'And what were you before you took on this exciting job, Mr Thothadri?', I asked.

'I was senior filing clerk. The junior clerk spread false and malicious rumours about me. I will not sully your ears with what exactly he told the manager. But both of them joined hands in a conspiracy against me and got me transferred to this job, six months ago. But it's all for the good, I suppose. I have enough time now to read a chapter from the Ramayana in the office every day. I have almost finished it and will start on the Mahabharata next, go on to the Vishnu Puranas and then the Bhagavatam. I hope to finish reading all of them again before I retire'

'In Tamil?'

'Of course, not', Thothadri was shocked. 'In Sanskrit, of course. I am a true Brahmin. In Tamil!' There was a wealth of disgust in that last phrase.

'I'm sorry, Mr Thothadri. My fault. I should have realised immediately that you are a Sanskrit pundit. By the way, Mr Kailasam said something about my working for a few days in every section, so that I would get to know what is done in each department. He said this is very important if I am to become an efficient and effective PRO.'

'A great man, Mr Kailasam is a great man', Thothadri crooned. He removed his spectacles and rubbed them dirty again with the edge of his dhoti. 'You know Mr Sharma, his grandfather started this bank. A great man, Mr Kailasam. He personally gave me a loan of three thousand rupees for my daughter's wedding. And no interest, not a single paisa. A very great man.'

I stared at Thothadri, my heart sinking to my ankle. The man was obviously senile. What kind of hell-hole had I got myself into?

'Yes Mr Kailasam is indeed a great man, even though he is my father-in-law......'

Thothadri laughed: cackled rather. 'Though he is my father-in-law', he cried, slapping his thigh and rocking to and fro, 'Though he is my father-in-law! A great joke! I can see you are a witty person, Mr Sharma. I think I am going to like you very much. But you must not crack jokes about the Chairman. Your might be suspended, or even dismissed if someone other than me hears you. They all carry tales, you see. But I don't, I swear I don't.' His voice rose shrilly, like a little boy denying that he stole the five-rupee coin on the kitchen table to buy ice cream. He calmed down and chuckled. 'But you are his son-in-law, you can say anything. He can dismiss you from the bank but not from his house. Only his daughter has the power to do that.' He cackled again and took off his spectacles again, this time to wipe the tears of merriment from his eyes.

I was getting desperate. 'Mr Thothadri, have there been any instructions from the Chairman's office about my training?' I was almost shouting.

'No need to shout, you know', Thothadri muttered, his head hung low, filled with shame that he, a veteran bank employee of 35 years experience, was being shouted at by a youngster who had joined only that day. 'I'm old enough to be your father. This is the problem with the younger generation—no respect for age.' He looked as if he was going to cry.

The next moment his mood changed to bubbling enthusiasm, almost joy. 'No Mr Sharma, I have received no instructions. But do not worry. I will train you myself. I will make you the best and greatest PRO this bank has seen. Together we will show that stupid Sankaralingam, that filing clerk who got me kicked here, what stuff we are made of, together...'

'Good God', I thought, 'He's a manic-depressive. I've got a madman for a boss.'

I tried to soothe him, calm him down. 'Yes, Mr Thothadri, yes, we'll be a great team. But that is a long-term project. What shall I do now?'

'To start with, Bharat...I hope you don't mind me calling you Bharat, though you are the Chairman's son-in-law and I am a poor filing clerk, I mean PRO...you are like a son to me.'

'I don't mind Mr Thothadri.'

'That is good Bharat; that is very good. I always felt that the younger generation today knows how to respect its elders. Give respect and take respect; that is my motto. Today you shall familiarise yourself with my office, I mean our office.'

Thothadri got up, scuttled around his desk and swept the pile of junk on the peon's table on to the floor.

'That is your table.' He pointed out proudly. 'The peon used to sit at it. One other job of this department, which I forgot to mention please forgive me, is to cut out references in the newspapers to our bank and to our competitors, paste them in separate scrapbooks and send them up to the Chairman's office. The peon does that job. We go fifty-fifty on the resale of newspapers. Payya, Payya. That peon, he is never in his seat. He's always running off somewhere else. I will make him clean the table for you later. Meanwhile, in deference to the Chairman's wishes, why don't you move around the other departments and get to know people? I'll get along with the Valmiki Ramayana.'

***

I went straight home. Renu, in her dressing gown, opened the door. I ranted and raved. My life had been ruined, I shouted. I picked up the sofa cushions in the living room and threw them out into the garden. I could not, utterly refused to, sit a moment in that rat hole with that lunatic. I smashed a flower vase against the wall. Who did they think I was? Was I a doctor of English Literature or a moron and an imbecile? I lifted a chair and was about to throw it at a gilt-edged mirror when Renu grabbed me. She threw her arms around me from behind and dragged me back. I dropped the chair and stood still, rage and despair pulsing outward from my brain and pounding at my skull.

Renu slipped around me, still holding me. She soothed me. Soon I was calm enough to hear what she was saying. 'I'm sorry darling, I'm sorry darling.' She kept repeating, like a litany against fear. She promised me that I would immediately be made Public Relations Manager, a new post would be created for me. Within two days, I would have an office suite on the tenth floor, next to her father's. She would personally choose the decor and the furnishings. She would make sure that I got a pretty secretary and efficient staff.

'I desperately want you to be happy Bharat. I'll make you happy.' As an immediate lollipop, she undid the buttons of her dressing gown, under which she was wearing nothing, and her lush breasts tumbled out. She tightened her arms around my neck and pressed herself against me, breasts with already hard nipples crushed against my chest, pelvis against pelvis, and began to move and writhe. Heat exploded within me and I kissed her mouth, her face, her ears, squeezed her breasts hard, sucked ferociously at her nipples, groaning in my need for a mind-blowing orgasm. 'Come, darling, come', she moaned. 'Here, now.' We sank to the carpet.

* * *

Things improved a little after that. I had a plush office, with two air-conditioners, a huge rosewood desk and a secretary in the ante-room. A shining brass plate on the door announced to the world that I was the Public Relations Manager. I had two assistants, glorified errand boys who called themselves Public Relations Officers, to boss around.

But that was all. I never really got around to getting to know how a bank really worked. I would, of course, drop in on managers of other departments. But they always fobbed me off, giving me a few basic details about their work and then calling for the inevitable cup of coffee that always had too much sugar in it. It was the interminable round of coffees that finally stopped me trying to find out more about how the bank worked.

I tried to assign myself more work but came up against a blank wall. The private sector banks did not want intimate contact with the public: the less the public knew about the bank, the better the banker liked it. I had no work. Thothadri could have done my job.

My secretary, a pretty, fluffy, bird-brained Anglo-Indian girl, spent the whole day polishing her fingernails and reading Barbara Cartland and Mills and Boon novels. I once quoted P G Wodehouse to her: 'If your brains were made of silk, Miss Adie, there wouldn't be enough to stitch a pair of cami-knickers for a canary.' She giggled and simpered, 'Oh, Sir, how kind of you to say so.' My PROs made files of clippings from the newspapers and kept applying once a month for a transfer. Some afternoons, the four of us locked the doors and played rummy at my rosewood desk. I tried to teach them bridge but it was no use. Miss Adie could not master even poker. Soon, it was only 'three cards'. I was smoking heavily, up to fifty cigarettes a day and four 'chhota pegs' became mandatory in the evening before dinner.

Renu became pregnant two months after we got married and refused to let me make love to her. 'It might harm the baby, darling.' I accepted with such misery on my face that she laughed, patted my cheek, and said, 'It's for less than a year darling, so, don't look so morose. Cheer up!'

Cheer up, bloody hell!

By the time my first child was born—we named him Lakshman—I began to get attacks of depression. I was irritable, morose, silent for long spells, smoked seventy cigarettes a day and my drinking went up terrifyingly. I would drink half-a-bottle of anodyne vodka sitting alone in my 'study'—that was another joke, I hadn't read a book in months—and stay cold sober.

Four months after my son was born, Renu became pregnant again. It was almost as if she wanted to be done with her duty of bearing children and get on with more important work. She was now totally self-sufficient. I was no more than an appendage, almost vestigial. I was convinced that, as far as she was concerned, I had performed my duties and there was no other use for me. The conviction became stronger when I stumbled across a book that she had bought before we were married. It was a basic text-book on genetics, well-worn and extensively underlined and annotated, with notes in Renu's neat, small handwriting, the type ideal for writing in ledgers. She had married me to revitalise the family strain, bringing in new genes: this time of a highly-evolved, intellectual type.

The final proof came after our daughter, Hamsini was born. Without consulting me, she got herself sterilised. No more children. And no more sex either. As I told you, her sexual drive had always been weak, it was only a means to many ends. I was also finding it difficult to perform effectively: an expended and thrown away tool cannot stand up easily again. She decided we would sleep in separate bedrooms, 'since the children might disturb your sleep'. I did not bother to point out that the children slept with an ayah.

She plunged into a ferocious study of banking, flailing away at massive textbooks on accountancy, management, foreign exchange transactions, the international monetary system and the history of Indian banking. She spent most of her time in her 'study' or in her father's suite at the bank. She had a permanent desk there. After ensuring posterity, she was going for her goal, the first woman chief executive of a bank in our country.

The crowning irony came when I discovered that my colleagues at the bank had given the acronym PRM a different expansion: To them, I was the Pubic Relations Manager. I emptied a bottle of Scotch brooding over this, but finally I went to bed laughing. Pubic was okay, but where were the relations?

My father-in-law rarely visited us. Whenever he did, he played with his grandchildren and left within half an hour. I was getting desperate. One day, it became bad enough for me to stop him as he was leaving our house and ask him: 'Sir, would you please consider releasing me from the condition that I should work only in your bank? After all, I am not doing much in the PR department.'

'Nonsense', he growled, 'The PR department is an important, indeed vital, aspect of the bank. That section I will never again depute to anyone outside the family. And I will repeat what I said the first time that we met: I'll be damned if I have a school-teacher for a son-in-law.'

You may wonder why I just did not tell them all to go to hell and get back to being a teacher. I couldn't, not just then. For one thing, I loved my children too much and was convinced that they needed a father in the house. For another, I had lost my will, lost the power and even the desire to act as an individual; my ego had been watered down to a thin gruel which could fuel no action.

I tried another tack. I sent up a letter to Kailasam. I still remember, word for word, what I wrote: the mad, black humour of it.

'I have', the memo said, 'after four years in this venerable (not venereal, mind) money-lending institution, without any prodding or assistance whatsoever, from any person whomsoever, based my mental process on the Cartesian dictum 'cogito, ergo sum' and the axioms of deductive logic encapsulated in the writings of Aristotle and Arthur Conan Doyle, come to the conclusion (Will none shout 'Eureka!'?) that public relations implies, some kind of relations with the public who, in the limited context of banking operations, primarily include the clients of this bank. As my cogitations have made it obvious that you alone have the genius to warm the cockles of, and win over, the hearts of the big slugs and the small depositors are not worth the time and the trouble (I can't imagine anything more yawn-making than small talk with a small depositor) I propose to make out a list of middle industrialists who are our clients, meet them personally, individually or at small, exclusive parties, and make them feel we love them more than their wives love their poodles. I hope and trust this little gem of mine has your consent and approval. Yours respectfully Bharat Sharma, Pubic Relations Manager PS: Note the new-old designation.'

Kailasam sent back a typed memo the next day: 'Damned right I'll tan your backside if you go near the big ones. As for the rest, do what you like as long as you don't fuck up anything. If you do, your arse is on the line.' It was signed with a flourish—just the letter 'K' which took up half the page.

And so, to get out of that depressing office as often as possible, I called on small and medium industrialists and traders, making friends with them and sending on their complaints and suggestions to Kailasam, who threw them away unread into the waste-paper basket.

There was one fellow to whom I became very close; personally, and not as the bank's PRM. He was Muthiah, a Chettiar who owned an engineering unit in the Guindy Industrial Estate and had plans of expanding into plastics and electronics. We seemed to be suited to each other very well. Both of us liked Bloody Marys, our golf handicap was 24 and it looked like we could play only with each other for the rest of our lives, since there was only a slim chance of it improving to 23; both of us liked classical jazz and analysing the future of the human mind and lolling on the sands of Marina beach till three o'clock in the morning.

He introduced me to horse racing. I started with small bets. He was deeply into it and was making quite a tidy amount. He taught me all the systems of calculating the chances of picking a winner, handicapping, timing, watching the track trials and the art of spotting whether a horse is in peak condition or not. He even forced me to read a book on horses written by a veterinarian. He taught me the science and art of bribing jockeys and trainers and fixing races. I got caught up in the madness, and a profitable madness it was. Soon my minimum bet was a thousand rupees. We were lucky too and some long shots paid off, though we had the usual share of favourites being beaten by a short head. When my first season at the Madras races ended, I had won about thirty thousand rupees. By that time, Muthu and I had become almost inseparable.

Sunday nights we went on a boozing binge, starting usually at the Madras Race Club and ending up on Marina beach around two in the morning. One Sunday, we left the race club and were driving down Mount Road, trying to decide where we would settle for the evening, when Muthu said 'Bharat, I haven't told anyone this. I have two serious problems to sort out now. One is my industry. It is not doing well, but it is a temporary phase, I am sure. Cash flow problems caused by the power cuts, demand bottlenecks and a little labour trouble. It's not too serious. I can hold on but it is affecting my expansion plans. The company needs a blood transfusion of about two crores of rupees. Electronics is the wave of the future. There is nothing you cannot do in electronics. I realised this the last time I went to the United States. India cannot afford to and will not ignore the electronics revolution. Take computers, for instance. But....'

'But', I interrupted, 'I can't help you in any way, friend.'

'Why not, you're the Chairman's son-in-law.'

'That's why not. It is precisely because I am the Chairman's son-in-law that my recommendation would be the worst thing that could happen to you. Not only would your request be rejected, he might even call in the loans he has given you.'

'It's that way, is it? No matter. I'll find a way out. Maybe I'll tell him what a creep you are and he'll open the vaults for me.'

'What's the other problem?'

'It's my wife.'

'You too?'

'What do you mean, you too?'

'I mean, me too. But go on with your problem.'

'You know that I am an engineering graduate with an MBA degree. My interests are limited. Professionally my only interests are my factory and my business. Outside of it, racing and boozing. We married very young, as often happens in Chettiar families. I was twenty-three and she was seventeen. It was a marriage of convenience, to keep the gold jewellery and share certificates within the family. Both of us have been very happy, except for one thing. She continued her education after we got married. I wanted her to keep herself occupied. She got an MA in philosophy and another in literature. She's an expert in Carnatic, Hindustani, and Western Classical music. She's bored and I don't know how to help. She's a freak. Imagine an intellectual Chettiar! We are a tribe of money-grubbers and our minds don't break out of the rupee-paise circle. She doesn't have anybody interesting to talk to, since our social circle is limited to other businessmen and their mutton-headed wives. So she's bored, irritable, unhappy; little things make her fly into a temper and the tension is building between us. We don't have children either, and that's not for want of trying.'

'Maybe I could help'

'That's what I thought. You are the intellectual type, both of you will hit it off wonderfully, I'm sure.'

'Why didn't you tell me this stuff earlier? I would have been happy to help out.'

'I didn't think of it till now. So, how about lunch next Sunday at my house?'

'Fine, I will look forward to it.'

'What about your wife?'

'Oh, forget her, she lives her life and I live mine and it looks like the twain will never meet again. See, that's poetry for you.'

'Okay, I won't bring it up again unless you do.'

'Fine, let's keep it that way for now. One day soon, I may unburden myself too. Now, drive this chariot of yours to the Connemara. I'm bloody thirsty.'

* * *

Muthu's wife, Uma. I am eternally grateful to her. She gave me back my individuality, my ego. The next Sunday, Muthu and I decided to drop the racecourse and spend the whole afternoon at home. Uma and Muthu were waiting on the porch as I drove into the driveway and walked up to them.

'Uma, this is Dr Bharat Sharma, a good friend of mine. He is the PR manager of the Bank. Bharat, Uma my wife.'

She must have been around twenty six, plump, dark and pretty and slightly tall for a South Indian woman. She wore no make-up except lipstick. There was a languor about her, a hint of the boredom seeping through.

'Namaskaram.' We moved to cane chairs near the French window opening out on to a manicured lawn. The room was tastefully decorated and furnished, a delicate combination of pastel shades on the walls, on which were hung reproductions of Goya, Picasso and El Greco. There was a piano in one corner of the huge drawing room.

'Beer, Bharat?' Muthu asked, indicating that this afternoon we were going light on the booze.

With an ice-cold glass of Kingfisher in my hand, I started discoursing on El Greco. A sparkle of interest flashed out of Uma's eyes and it grew into an aura that lit up her face as I opened the sluices of the conversation, or rather my discourse, and let it flow swiftly. It moved from art to Oscar Wilde to 'Nature imitates Art' to 'nothing to declare but my genius', to the nature of literary genius, to Eliot, to 'Tradition and the Individual Talent' and I could see Uma becoming more and more excited. Muthu refilled the beer glasses.

'You know, Uma, our friend Bharat is the antithesis of the peacock; he projects the dull grey aura of the banker to hide his true, and brilliantly flashing colours. Did you know that he was a professor of English before he married Renu, Kailasam's daughter, and joined the bank?'

'Dr Bharat Sharma?' Uma sat upright and leaned forward, excitement and wonder dancing in her face. 'Of Presidency College?'

I stood up, clicked my heels and ripped of a Teutonic bow. 'The same, Ma'am.'

Uma laughed and clapped her hands. 'How wonderful. Oh Doctor, we heard so much about your brilliant lectures when I was in Stella Maris College. I was dying for a chance to listen to you. Now I will be able to listen to you in my own house. Won't those old classmates of mine be jealous?'

'I doubt the green-eyed monster will smite them so hard, Mrs. Muthiah. I've given up all that. I am rusting away as a mere public relations manager now.'

'What's all this Dr Sharma, Mrs. Muthiah rubbish', Muthu broke in.' You can't be so formal. From now on it is Bharat and Uma, my orders, understand?'

'Oh no, I couldn't. He is a guru.'

'As I told you, Uma, I am a guru no longer. And I would be honoured if you thought of me as your friend and called me Bharat. Is it a deal?' I put out my hand and Uma took it shyly. 'It's a deal, Bharat.' I toasted our friendship with a fresh glass of beer.

Uma stood up. 'You are not a strict vegetarian, I hope, Bharat. My mother sent me some excellent tiger prawns.'

'I love prawns, Uma.'

'Lovely, now will you please excuse me? I want to cook those prawns myself.'

After a superb lunch during which I ate twice what I normally do, we drifted back to the living room and I flopped on a soft, deep settee.

'Well, if Uma won't mind....'

'Sure, go ahead, Bharat, relax.'

I flipped my shoes off and lay back with a groan of delicious repletion.

The phone rang. Muthu picked it up and within seconds his face twisted in annoyance. He rapped out a few sharp questions, said he would come over immediately and hung up.

'Damn and double damn. There's been a minor breakdown at the factory. I'm sorry Uma, Bharat, but I have to go. No, don't get up. Stay and talk to Uma. Hopefully, I'll be back in a couple of hours. I'll go and change into my workingman's outfit.'

After Muthu left, still cursing his luck, Uma drew her chair near the settee I was lying on. 'Okay Bharat, talk and I'll listen.'

I don't remember what I talked about that afternoon except that we rediscovered Life, the Universe and Everything. It was a revelation to me, a journey into my prehistoric past. Within what seemed to me to be minutes, the grandfather clock in the hall sounded five reverberating bongs.

Uma jumped up. 'Coffee, Bharat?'

'That would be lovely, but make mine black, please. My tummy is still engorged on that Cordon Bleu feast.'

We had coffee under a beach umbrella on the lawn. It was a mild evening and a gentle breeze played softly.

'Bharat, you said you would be honoured if I were your friend. Well, I am, now. And as a friend I must ask you a question which you should have asked yourself, but haven't . Why don't you go back to teaching?

The gentle breeze stopped ruffling my hair. The air was still. I held my breath. The birds stopped chattering. Stasis gripped the Universe. I laughed.

'Why don't I go back to teaching? I believe I will.'

Freedom was as simple as that. Two sentences. Uma had given me the gift of life. Symbolically I extended my left forefinger and she touched it with her right forefinger.

Excerpts from

'Les Cahiers du Bharat Sharma'

**Envy**

*A wonderful bird is the crow,*

*He flies where I'd love to go.*

*He does with élan*

*What I dearly wish I can:*

*Go splat, splat on the people below.*

# Chapter 8

*'God's in his Heaven...'*

—Robert Browning

Dr Hekyll and Mr Jyde stood thoughtfully, as I smoked a cigarette and took a walk around in my mind before continuing with my story. They seemed to have realised I needed a break, for they looked at each other and nodded. Mr Jyde bowed to Dr Hekyll, a gesture that he should take over.

'Bharat,' said Dr Jekyll, 'I know what you are going to say next. I know that you are going to say the fairy tales have got it all wrong; that nobody lives happily ever after.'

'But how? ... But how?' I spluttered.

'You still haven't got used to the idea of us,' said Mr Jyde. 'We are, you must always remember, parts of your mind.

And we know what is going on in there, much better than you do.'

'If you know everything about me, why do you want to listen to the story of my life?'

'It's the other way around. We want you to tell us your story.'

'So that,' said Dr Hekyll, 'you can begin to understand what you are all about.'

'You've lost me, guys.'

'Never mind,' said Dr Hekyll, lightly brushing my frontal lobe. 'You were going to say that the fairy tales have got it wrong; nobody lives happily ever after. You are tired, you need a break. So listen to me for a while. I will tell you a story. Listen to it and decide whether what you feel about fairy tales is a correct appreciation of the reality of human life.'

Dr Hekyll gathered his thoughts for a moment and told me the story of VSV:

Vadapathimangalam Srinivasaraghavan Venkatavaradan, VSV to all the world except his wife, who as a good Brahmin wife, addressed him either in the second person plural or as 'what is written on my forehead', pushed his bicycle up the flyover in dyspneal agony. He was, as he often told the mirror while he shaved in the mornings, fat, forty-eight and a failure. He was five and a half feet tall and looked equally broad. He had worked fifteen hours that day and he was tired and he did not have the energy to pedal up the flyover.

So he pushed his bicycle and the asthmatic wheeze that was his normal breathing moved up one full octave, like the diva hitting the high note in *Madame Butterfly*. He was bloody angry and the anger poured out of him in all directions, like the sweat that spurted from his pores. The soft wash of the full moon bathed a restlessly sleeping Delhi, but it did not cool VSV's heated bulk or tamp down the explosive rage within him. Though it was nearly one o'clock in the morning, the concrete surface of the flyover still radiated the intense heat it had soaked up during the day, when the temperature had crossed 48 degrees Centigrade.

'Enough is enough,' shouted VSV to the purposely deaf Universe as he reached the top of the flyover. He threw his bicycle down on the road. A sense of power coursed through him as his brain registered the grand defiance of his act. He felt glorious. He glared in triumph at the fallen bicycle which had metamorphosed into the avatar of all the injustice of an unjust world. At that moment, the bicycle represented his perennially snide boss, the whining sarcasm of his wife, the selfish demands of his five children, the month-end search for possibly forgotten one-rupee coins under the steel almirah and the threatened violence of the Pathan moneylender. He had an overwhelming desire to jump up and down on the bicycle, crushing, like the conquering hero, evil and injustice out of existence; but he remembered in the nick of time, the scatological abuse of the moneylender to whom he would have to go to get the money to repair the bicycle.

VSV sighed deeply and hitched his ample buttocks over the railing of the flyover. 'VSV,' he told himself, 'you can't win in this game.' He pulled out a cigarette and put it in his mouth. As he struck a light, he remembered that the doctor had told him to 'give it up or else...' But insurrection surged through him again and he lit his cigarette and extinguished the match with a masterful flick of the wrist. He drew in the smoke and exhaled, but not contentedly.

'Enough is enough,' he muttered as he thought of the way his boss, Rameshwar Anand, a deputy secretary in the industries ministry of the central government, had just that day found a new way to torture him.

Around half past four, VSV had gone into Anand's room with an armful of files marked 'Urgent'. Anand was chatting and laughing with two women lounging on the sofas in the 'conversation area'. The women were young and sexy, dressed in tight jeans and tops with plunging necklines that revealed the upper slopes of their substantial, proudly uplifted breasts. Trying not to disturb them, VSV left the files on Anand's desk and was moving towards the door when Anand called out: 'Hey, just a minute, you.'

VSV turned, just in time to catch Anand winking conspiratorially at the women. 'Here comes another hot rod up my you-know-what,' VSV thought, composing his face into the expression of soulful martyrdom which he put on whenever he sensed that Anand was about to launch what he called a humorous broadside, but what was really a vicious exercise of the authority emanating from a superior position in the government.

'Yes, sir?' VSV asked politely.

'My friend, colleague and minion,' Anand said with a grin, 'I'd like you to meet two very good friends of mine, Miss Shanti Mishra and Mrs. Rama Dayal.' One of the women waved a languid hand and the other uttered a bored 'Hi'.

'Ladies,' said Anand pointing at VSV, 'this is my private secretary, Vadapathimangalam Srinivasaraghavan Venkatavaradan'

The three of them burst into hysterical laughter. VSV stood still.

'His long name does not bother him. As you can see, his body is big enough to accommodate all three words and more.' Again they roared with laughter until tears came out of their eyes.

VSV turned and walked towards the door.

'Don't run away. I am not done with you yet. Not that you are capable of running.' The women giggled and the Mishra female piped up: 'Oh, Rameshwar, you are too wicked.' Anand smirked at them.

Anand got up and moved towards VSV. 'The secretary wants a detailed note on components imported by the electronics industry over the past three years. He wants it on his table tomorrow morning. I'll be dictating about ten pages. But I don't have the time now. These delicate bundles of femininity (more giggles from the sofa) have come all the way from Bombay and are going back early tomorrow. I have to take them shopping and feed their lovely mouths later. We'll be dining in the Mandarin restaurant. I'll come back after dinner and dictate the note. You'll have to type it up before you leave tonight. I'll have a look at it tomorrow and send it to the secretary. You may go now.'

VSV was a good Brahmin, which meant that his vocabulary of abuse was ten times bigger than that of the worst slum goonda. He let loose a cloacal flood as soon as he stepped out into the corridor and did not stop till he was back at his table. VSV had been able to leave his office only after midnight.

He finished the cigarette but could not summon up the energy to get up, pick up his cycle and pedal the remaining three miles to his three-room tenement.

'One more cigarette and I'll move,' he told himself and his thoughts turned to his wife Lakshmi, whose perennial complaint was that the only thing God had written on her forehead were the words 'Vadapathimangalam Srinivasaraghavan Venkatavaradan'.

She was eight years younger than VSV and still retained not only the physical bloom of youth but also its impatience and self-pity.

VSV had learned one lesson 27 years ago when he had joined the central government in Delhi as a stenographer. The lesson was that he was one amongst hundreds of millions of people in the world who were born losers, who never got the big chance, never struck it rich; they always moved two steps backward for every step forward. This is the way the world is, no bang, only an eternal whimper.

Lakshmi had never been able to understand this basic fact of life. Every waking moment she dreamed that one day she would dwell in marble halls, that they would be richer beyond the dreams of a poor Brahmin housewife. When she slept and her more unrealistic subconscious took over, she dreamt that they would at least have their own house, there would be enough money to run a car, enough money to hire a cook and a maid, to give the children a good education and send them to America, enough money for her to be bored and alleviate her boredom by buying two Kanchipuram silk saris at the same time.

VSV would not have minded it if she had only dreamt of these things. The trouble was that every morning she would insist on VSV sitting with her for half an hour and listening to a running commentary on what she had done in her dreams the previous night. This was her way, and a terrible way it was, of telling him that she hated everything about their life. It was her way of telling him that she held him solely responsible for the horrible hole they were in, a hole so deep and dark that they would all die without having lived for a moment in the bright sunshine that filled the lives of the Mehras and Guptas and Khannas and Kapoors who lived in Vasant Vihar and Greater Kailash and Sardar Patel Marg.

VSV saw no way of getting out of the hole and so he raved and ranted at Lakshmi. He sometimes got drunk on cheap liquor and made matters worse for himself. He drowned in self-piteous anger when he was drunk. The next day, he wallowed in self-piteous guilt, to cleanse which he scraped the barrel and bought Lakshmi a cotton sari. The saris were cheap but they were too expensive for his wallet. Ergo, repeated trips to the Pathan moneylender who charged interest at ten rupees per hundred per month, or 120 per cent per annum. Soon, like the government he served, he was borrowing to pay interest on past loans.

He could have, of course, made things more comfortable, even become rich, if he had accepted the bribes offered by industrialists and corporate liaison men who wanted copies of secret or confidential documents, license applications of their competitors, Cabinet notes ... the list was endless. VSV saw everyone around him raking in money under the table. But he remained strong. My honour is the only thing left to me, he told himself. They have stripped me of everything else. Let me at least keep my honour.

And so he took on part-time work as a job-typist. Luckily his father, who had been a stenographer in the Lok Sabha, had left him an old Remington typewriter. VSV often got up at four in the morning to type up material like the theses of Ph.D. students.

But the money was never enough. They had five children. Four daughters and a son. Two in college and three in school.

He stubbed out his cigarette and stood up with a sigh. He was still too tired to ride his bicycle. He stood there, breathing heavily.

And then it happened.

A jeep screeched to a halt near him. A bearded face peered out and a deep, mellifluous voice asked: 'Any problem? Can I help in any way?'

VSV was momentarily puzzled. A thought brushed the synapses of his brain that he had not heard the jeep drive up the flyover; how had it suddenly appeared at the top? But the thought was gossamer, a wisp that floated away as VSV peered suspiciously at the man in the jeep. One could never be sure these days and it was late in the night. The man could be one of those mad terrorists who might gun him down just for the pleasure of it.

But the man in the jeep was smiling pleasantly, eyebrows cocked in enquiry. Again he asked, in that deep and strangely soothing voice: 'Any problem? Can I help you?'

The man seemed genuinely keen to help and VSV was normally not impolite. But he had reached a kind of breaking point. A gust of fury swept through him again. He shook his fist in the man's face and shouted: 'No, you can't help. I have a thousand and one bloody problems and you can't help. The only effing way you can help is to give me two foreign cars, six houses in Delhi and five crores of rupees in cash. Can you do that? If not, bugger off and leave me in peace.'

The man nodded thoughtfully and smiled. 'Why not? In deserving cases our only aim is to please. Your three wishes are granted.' The man drove away.

It was past two in the morning when VSV got home. A sleepy Lakshmi opened the door and stumbled back into bed, muttering 'Your dinner's on the stove.' VSV swallowed a few mouthfuls of cold rice and thin rasam and went to bed. His thoughts dwelt for a few moments on the man in the jeep and his strange statement. 'A madman. Must have escaped from the lunatic asylum,' VSV mumbled and was fast asleep.

He was woken up by a continuous ringing of the doorbell. Lakshmi muttered, turned on her side and continued to sleep. Cursing inaudibly, VSV rose from his bed, put on the light and looked at his watch. It was five in the morning. 'Which stupid bastard can it be, disturbing us at this hour?', he grumbled as he went to the front door and opened it.

The jeep man stood there, the same pleasant smile on his face. Two bulky suitcases stood on the floor at his feet.

'Good morning,' said the man. 'Your three wishes are in these suitcases.' He smiled again and walked away quickly, not turning back when VSV shouted 'Hey, you there, what the hell is all this about?'

VSV tried to run after him but the man had disappeared. VSV walked back to his door and stared at the suitcases. Was this some kind of elaborate joke? What was all this nonsense about three wishes?

VSV jumped back suddenly. Was the man a terrorist after all? Oh God we're all going to be blown up!

But nothing happened. The suitcases squatted on the floor, innocent as the dawn that was breaking. VSV shuffled closer and peered at them as if he were Superman and could see what was inside with X-ray vision. He prodded the suitcases a couple of times with his right foot. They seemed quite heavy. He lifted one by the handle and shook it.

It seemed to be tightly packed. He tried the other one. This too was heavy and nothing rattled inside. VSV knelt on the floor and put his ear to the suitcases, one by one. No ticking sound. There did not seem to be a bomb inside.

He stood up, brushing the dust from his knees and scratched his nose. What now?

'What the hell,' VSV thought. 'Workers of the world unite; you have nothing to lose but your chains. If these boxes blow up my skull, what have I to lose but my headaches?' He hefted the suitcases, took them into the house and put them on the bed. He locked the front door, went back to the bed and stared at the suitcases. He squared his shoulders and with one jerky movement tried the catch on one of the suitcases. It was not locked.

VSV opened it. It was packed with bundles of five hundred rupee notes.

'The third wish. There must be one hundred thousand five hundred rupee notes', VSV thought.

He opened the other suitcase. More bundles of five hundred rupee notes. 'Couldn't fit them all in one box, I suppose.' Underneath, there were legal looking documents, each set neatly tied with red ribbons. He untied one set and glanced through the papers. There were title deeds making him the owner of a house in a 3,000 square yard plot in Vasant Vihar.

VSV's hands shook as he untied the other documents. They gave him ownership of two equally big houses on Aurangzeb Road and Amrita Shergil Marg, a five-bedroom duplex flat in Greater Kailash and a ten-acre farm between Mehrauli and Gurgaon. And there were registration certificates in his name for a Mercedes 600 and a Ferrari sports car. Two sets of keys for the cars winked at him from the bottom of the suitcase.

And then VSV noticed the visiting card pasted on the inner lid of the suitcase. It read: Compliments of: Adisesha, manager, Garuda Atman Management Service Private Limited. Proprietor; Mahavishnu. Address: Vaikuntham.

VSV sat absolutely immobile for five minutes, as if seized by an attack of catalepsy. Then he shook himself and laughed. He shook Lakshmi roughly and shouted: 'Wake up. Get up. See what I have got.'

Lakshmi twisted away from him and muttered irritably: 'Why can't the old goat allow a woman to sleep in peace? Work, work, work all day and not a moment's rest all night.'

'Wake up, you silly bitch. We're RICH,' roared VSV and dumped handfuls of the five hundred rupee bundles on her.

Lakshmi jumped up with a scream and stared at the notes. 'Oh my God, Hare Krishna, what have you done you old fool! You've gone and robbed a bank.'

'Shut up, woman, and listen,' VSV shouted. Lakshmi fell silent. He told her what had happened, words pouring out and stumbling over each other so that he was often incomprehensible.

'Thank the Lord,' Lakshmi whispered. 'It is all his Maya.' Her face lit up with savage excitement and glee. 'We are rich. We are rich. Good people always get their reward. I shall go immediately to the Ganesa temple in Vinay Nagar and break a coconut.'

'Oh Lord,' VSV groaned, raising his face to the ceiling. 'You dump crores of rupees in our laps and the woman wants to break one coconut, just one single, measly coconut. Go and break a dozen coconuts, woman. On second thought, half a dozen will do. We don't want the Lord to get indigestion, do we?'

And he started chuckling, whinnying, laughing, choking as little fingers of happy insanity plucked at the edges of his mind.

VSV stuffed his wallet with five hundred rupee notes and told Lakshmi to put the deeds to the Vasant Vihar house in her handbag. He repacked the suitcases and pushed them under the bed. They said nothing to the children who were waking up just then. After they had left for school and college, they settled down to a long and happy argument about how to keep the money safe. They finally decided they would follow the principle of the 'Purloined Letter'. The suitcases would remain under the bed for the time being.

VSV and Lakshmi took a taxi to Vasant Vihar. This was the second time in their lives they travelled in a taxi. The first was 15 years earlier when Lakshmi had to be rushed to the hospital with acute appendicitis. Throughout the drive they sat ramrod stiff, leaning forward to grip the front seat, too tense to lean back. What if it were all a great, cruel hoax? What if the chowkidar set the dogs on them? What if they went back home and found that the currency notes were only pieces of newspaper?

They stopped the taxi a hundred yards away from the house in Vasant Vihar and walked timidly forward. But they need not have worried. There was a chowkidar at the gate and his face lit up as he saw them. He ushered them politely down the curving drive to the porch where a beautiful, immaculately dressed young woman greeted them with a dazzling smile.

It was no hoax. It was all true. It had all happened. They were rich; rich beyond even the dreams of Lakshmi. They went on a holiday abroad. A week in London, two weeks in Paris and then on to New York, Washington and Los Angeles. The children were admitted to schools and colleges in the United States. VSV and Lakshmi sailed back to India on a leisurely cruise through Hawaii, Tokyo, Hong Kong, Bangkok and Singapore.

Dr Hekyll paused and looked at me expectantly. I knew what I had to say.

'Let me finish the story,' I said. 'VSV was arrested by the Central Bureau of Investigation on the charge of a government servant having assets disproportionate to his known sources of income. The trial would not have lasted long. The only witness who could have saved VSV was Adisesha, manager, Garuda Atman Management Services Private Limited; Prop: Mahavishnu. But Adisehsha was in Vaikuntam i.e. Heaven. God's in his Heaven. The judge convicted VSV and sent him to jail for ten years.'

Dr Hekyll and Mr Jyde looked at each other. Mr Jyde said: 'That is what happens, if that is the way you want the story to end. The choice is yours. After all, it was you who kept insisting that the fairy tales have got it wrong, that nobody lives happily ever after.'

# Chapter 9

*If happiness is a winning bet, the punter is the true Karma Yogi. He gets drunk after the races, celebrating his winnings or drowning his sorrows.*

—'The Collected Aphorisms of the Unknown Punter'

'It's not a question of how I want it. What is the use of a story with a moral that depends on the personal fancy of an individual?' I asked Dr Hekyll and Mr Jyde.

They laughed.

'The moral of any parable lies both in the tongue of the teller and the ear of the listener', said Dr Hekyll. 'And the moral may change according to the ideology of the tongue and the received wisdom of the ear.'

'Everything is true. And nothing is true, to paraphrase the Great Detective,' said

Mr Jyde, in the voice of Peter Ustinov playing Hercule Poirot.

I laughed. 'Okay let's cut the crap. You told me one story. I'll tell you one. Incidentally, this really happened and it happened to me, so it is true as far as I am concerned. And the moral of this story does not depend on my tongue or your ears.'

'Pray proceed; continue. Your narrative will interest us strangely,' said Mr Jyde, now assuming the voice of Peter Cushing playing Sherlock Holmes.

I went to my desk and took out a notebook.

'I wrote it all down, hoping that one day I would publish a book of short stories,' I said and sat down to read to them the story of a day at the horse races.

I tore the betting card in two (I read aloud) and matched the halves and tore them across, matched the quarters and tore them again and continued till I had a handful of stiff, little pieces of pasteboard: the relics of modest greed. I cupped them in my hands and threw them in the air. A puff of wind caught the scraps and lifted them high, where they rocked for a moment and floated gracefully down to the hunched shoulders of the crowd, shuffling towards the betting ring of the Bangalore racecourse.

Rosinante. The name should have warned me. No storyteller will draw a moral in the second paragraph of his tale, but there is no harm in dropping little gems of wisdom on the way. Today's lesson is: education isn't worth a damn. I have taught literature but I backed a horse called Rosinante! The aged mare had finished eleventh in a field of twelve. She did not finish twelfth because one of the runners had broken a foreleg while turning for home and had to be destroyed.

It was not stupidity that had blocked my subconscious from making the association with Don Quixote's mount and warning me off the bet. Nor had it been a wild gambler's throw. There had been reasons for backing the nag, reasons which had seemed sound enough when I placed what was for me a 'life's bet' of a hundred rupees, at odds of thirty to one.

The previous day, I had been sipping a studious beer or six in the bar of the Bangalore Press Club, staring at the track trials section of the Original Vel racing guide with that blank-eyed, empty-minded concentration that most punters believe is a sure way of picking winners. Suddenly, a heavy hand thumped my back and a rum-hoarsened voice grated 'Salam Aleikum, Bharat Sahib.'

As I twisted to rub my stinging back, Ibrahim, sports reporter and sometimes substitute racing correspondent of the *Indian Herald,* lowered himself into the chair next to mine.

Ibrahim's manners are as gross as he is fat; his speech is as lacking in humility as his shaven head is of hair. His intelligence is as massive as his bulk; only his brain is an adding machine that cannot look beyond rupees and paise. Nobody knew how anybody could be near him without wanting to be somewhere else, but no one had the moral courage or strength of personality to walk away from him; we were like rabbits hypnotised by a snake.

With what he considered to be a friendly grin, twisting his face into grotesquely separate lumps of cheeks, lips, nose and jowls, he said: 'Salam Aleikum, Bharat Sahib. Just the fellow for whom I was looking.'

'You came, you saw, you push off,' I growled, desperately trying to fight the rabbit complex.

'Waiter,' he bellowed, 'a beer and a large rum.'

Ibrahim snatched the racing guide from my hands, placed it on the table and leaned forward: 'Study that crap till the horses are lined up for the Derby and you still won't pick a winner. I'll give you one, only one; you can back your trousers and shirt on it and go home to Madras rich for the next two weeks. She's been prepared over the last few months just for this race tomorrow. The odds won't open at less than 30 to one, they'll be backed down to sixes and she'll walk the race.'

He leaned back, smiling like a guru who had shown his disciplines how to unlock the gates of Heaven with nothing but a prayer and a diet of goat's milk and groundnuts, spiced with lashings of sex with unwashed American neurotics.

The beer and the rum arrived. Ibrahim waited till I had filled my glass and raised his. 'Cheers, long life.' I grunted, lifted the glass forehead-high and lowered it for a deep draught of ice-cold beer.

'OK, what's the name of the horse?' I asked, the rabbit once again.

'Rosinante in the seventh race, the penultimate one.' Anyone would have said second-last, but Ibrahim was an Anglomaniac. He boasted often enough that he was one of ten people in India who really knew the English language, usually adding that these 10 did not include R K Narayan, Shashi Tharoor and George Fernandes, but did include a Bengali professor of English Literature in the North Eastern Hill University and a superintendent in the social welfare department of the Tamil Nadu government.

'Rosinante?', I shouted, incredulous. 'Rosinante?'

'Sshh', Ibrahim whispered fiercely, 'don't broadcast my hard-earned tip to the whole world. Do you want the odds to plummet? Yes, Rosinante. Why not Rosinante? Didn't Mother's Boy win the Invitation Cup?'

If there was one thing that Ibrahim did not admit to being—and it was a rare confession—it was to being a practical joker. Therefore, I had to figure out what his angle was. I needed time. I lifted my glass and took another long pull at the beer; slowly pulled out a cigarette from the packet of Charminar Specials on the table and took my time lighting it, inhaling deeply and blowing the smoke out slowly to extinguish the burning matchstick and putting it in the ash tray. All the while Ibrahim watched, tensely I thought, with a frown on his face, trying to gauge whether the fish was nibbling at the bait. For, it was a bait: Ibrahim never volunteered anything.

'How many rums have you had this evening?'

'Look, moron,' Ibrahim continued in the same fierce whisper, 'I can understand why you are so sceptical. All the world and its grandmother know that the owner is running the nag in the races only to get the feed subsidy from the Race Club.' He had forgotten his injunction to talk softly. The words were gushing out in a voice that grew louder with each syllable.

'Sshh', I mimicked his angry whisper, 'Do you want the odds to go down?'

'You're right', he whispered, looking all around to check whether anyone had been listening to him. I could now believe it. The man was serious. Ibrahim gulped some more rum and pulled out a handkerchief and wiped his face.

'It's a coup', he intoned, in a tone of voice that Indira Gandhi would have used when she announced to her cronies that she was going to impose the Emergency.

He waited for a reaction, a gasp of surprise, of wonder, perhaps. I did not oblige him.

'Haven't you heard of coups in racing? This is only my fifth rum. I got the tip from the chief syce to the trainer, Mohammed Osman. He wouldn't talk until I gave him an IOU for a bottle of army rum. The owner, Salim Mushtaq, is Osman's brother-in-law. And Salim is my mother's third cousin's husband's brother. And he told my father that he was going to back 20,000 bucks with the Bombay bookies, 15 minutes before the race starts. It has all been arranged. All the other jockeys have been fixed. Rosinante will hit the front and keep going. The other jockeys will sit with strangleholds on their mounts and a couple will make a late bid when the race is practically over. Do you believe me now?'

'Thanks a lot, Ibrahim. Can I have some peace now? I haven't yet worked out my jackpot combination for tomorrow. Since I am going to invest only 60 rupees, it needs a lot of concentration. You of all people should know that one cannot concentrate in company. So, I'll be obliged if you will push off.' I picked up the racing guide and moved my chair to turn my back on him.

Ibrahim swigged some more rum and sighed: 'That's the way the world is. Try to do a guy a favour and he spits on your face.'

Actually, it was Ibrahim who had been spitting on my face. When he gets excited, he exudes a fine salivary spray which rides on the flood of words.

'Ah', I said, turning to face him, 'now I am beginning to believe you.'

It was the word 'favour' that had tipped me off. Ibrahim never gave away something for nothing.

'What do you want me to do?'

Ibrahim put on a pained expression. It was wonderful watching his version of injured innocence which involved wrinkling his brow, screwing up his eyes, letting his mouth droop and making two of his three chins wobble. This was the time to be careful. Whenever he put on that act it meant he felt he had you hooked.

'Don't be crude', he boomed. 'You should observe the forms of courteous bargaining. You, if you had any sensibility, would have allowed me to broach the subject with taste, with charm ...'

'Cut the bullshit. Tell me what you want from me. If it is important enough for you, I'll believe the race is fixed for Rosinante to win.'

'OK, have it your way, though it is repugnant to me to operate without style. You do not seem to realise that style is everything; without style we are but beasts of the field and brutes of the forest, rutting our way through a short earthly life without hope of divine grace ... OK, OK, I'll get to the point. You remember the two-part article I wrote on stud farms? Your cousin, that son-of-a-bitch Paapaan accounts manager, Ramachandra Iyer, is questioning the bill of expenses I sent in. I want you to use your influence, I mean your good offices, to get it passed.'

'How much was the bill for?'

'Two thousand five hundred.'

'The bill was padded by a thousand, I suppose?'

'Of course it was. Wouldn't you do it? I mean, wouldn't you screw the most out the leeches that own the paper? Everyone does it. Why shouldn't I? '

Ibrahim was shouting now. All heads were turned towards us. Every journalist, in a bar or outside, loves to watch a fight. Gore is news.

'Son,' I said, putting on a voluminous cloak of condescension, gloriously happy that Ibrahim had given me an opening to practice gobs of one-upmanship on him, a rare opportunity. 'You are a backchat at the game. Fleecing the Marwadi is a fine art, indeed a scientific art. Don't forget they have centuries of experience of shafting the other fellow; tightfistedness is almost a genetic trait with the guys who pay our salaries on the first of the month.'

I paused, enjoying my ascendancy. Ibrahim, to give him credit, sat still. He did not throw his rum glass at me. He did not let loose a barrage of abuse. He was an adept in the art of squeezing our Marwadi owners and did not have to sit through what was to him, an elementary lesson.

'I would have padded the bill by thousand five hundred, leaving room for bargaining and you would have been sure of atleast eight hundred to donate to the bookies. Don't worry, I'll do it. And I believe that Rosinante will win because you will sell your dying grandmother's catheter for ten bucks. And a stable boy's tip is far more valuable currency for you.'

'Thanks, Bharat.' Ibrahim finished his drink and stood up. 'Though, why I should thank you I don't know, particularly because of the last nasty bit and more so because ours is a business deal. It is my essential good nature, I suppose, the vastness of which is immeasurable, as is well-known among the cognoscenti, ' Now that he had got what he wanted, Ibrahim was his usual insufferable self again.

He moved towards the door, away from the bar counter. I waited till he had taken a dozen steps.

''Ibrahim', I called out.

He turned and rolled back to the table.

'The bar counter is in the other direction,' I said, not looking up at him but studying the racing guide. 'Pay for the rum and the beer. As you said, ours is a business deal.'

The other omens too had been propitious. The attractiveness of Ibrahim's tip had been enhanced by the power of Numerology, or rather my interpretation of the science which every amateur racegoer believes is more powerfully prophetic than astrology.

Rosinante was to run in the seventh race. Write down the number 7. It was horse number 11. Therefore, 711. It was drawn number four. Thus 7114. The race was to be run at five in the evening. Ergo 71145, which was the phone number of the Malaysian-Indian college teacher, I had met at a party in Madras a few days earlier. The lady, like Barkis, appeared to be willing. And Rosinante spelled 71145.

That was not all. The *Indian Herald*'s tame astrologer, who wrote the column 'Star Trek' in the Sunday section, had advised Aquarians (I was born on January 31): 'Fortune and a fair one, go hand in hand. Don't look a gift horse in the mouth.'

The fair one was on her way; well, practically on her way; so why should not fortune, at least a small one, follow? And hadn't I been given a gift horse?

* * *

As I said, the name should have warned me. Also, the fair one was not really fair. She was rather dark, well OK, black as midnight. Her breasts threatened to burst out of her blouse every time she took a deep breath and her sari moulded itself around the lithe, long columns of polished granite that I imagined were her thighs. All this made her fair enough for me. The gift horse had turned into a Trojan Horse, fortune had shunted herself into a siding and the fair one might do the same. But there was always the Pathan moneylender and Jenny, the general manager's secretary.

I took a deep breath and pulled out my wallet. Five hundred rupees and two weeks to go for pay day. As I stuffed my wallet back into my hip pocket, I heard Ibrahim shouting: 'Where the hell were you? I looked all over but couldn't find you. This damned crowd. I wanted to tell you the coup was off. Rosinante was not 'on job'. I found out after the fifth race and have been hunting frantically for you. Did you back a lot?'

What he meant was 'Will my bill be cleared?'

'As you can see', I replied wearily, 'I still have my trousers and shirt on though I think my Y-fronts are missing. Ibrahim, the next time you want me to do something for you, don't make it a favour for a favour. I'll do anything for you if you will just stay away from me. Write a letter. Send a telegram.'

As I moved away, back stiff in anger but feeling more like an absurd marionette than a furious friend who had been stabbed in the back, I heard a soft voice call out 'Dr Bharat Sharma, a moment, if you please.'

It was my old friend Muthiah whom I had not met for years. 'Son of a bitch,' I shouted as we hugged each other, 'where the hell have you been all these years?'

Muthiah smiled at me: 'I should be asking that question. Uma was enquiring about you just the other day.'

'I'm sorry, Muthu. I should have come and seen you. I can never forget the two of you. You saved my life, remember?'

'Don't be melodramatic, Bharat. We didn't pull you out of a burning inferno or save you from drowning. In fact, you saved yourself. We only helped you over the last tough bit.'

'I disagree. The two of you are responsible for my rebirth, not that my second life has been a raving success.'

'Forget the past, chum.'

'How's Uma? Do you have any children?'

'I have two daughters and a son. We made up for the time lost in the first five years of our marriage.'

We grinned fondly at each other.

'How's the day been?' Muthu asked.

'Not too bad.' I blushed inwardly but I had no intention of revealing my idiocy in backing Rosinante. 'But not too good either. I wouldn't sneer at a good one in this race.'

'How much are you willing to back? All that you have in your wallet?'

'You have a tip that strong?'

'It's not a tip. It is my own coup. I have already backed thirty thousand with the Bombay bookies. I'm here to back another ten thousand in cash.'

'I'll empty my wallet and back four hundred. Which horse is it?'

'Centaur. Look, the odds on Centaur are now 20 to one, even 30 to one with some bookies. I want to spread the bet among seven or eight bookies. Will you help me?'

'Sure, what do you want me to do?'

Muthu pulled out 20 slim bundles of hundred rupee notes. There were six to a bundle, five hundred for the bet and a hundred for the betting tax. He gave me ten.

'Yet once more into the ring, dear friends. You move clockwise and I'll go the other way. Place bets with ever alternate bookie. We'll meet on the members' stand lawns.'

* * *

'The horses have reached the starting gate.' The commentator's voice was mournful, as if he disapproved of gambling but was forced into the racecourse to keep body and soul together; or as if he had bet huge amounts and lost; or as if he had a pain in the tummy —— doom, despair or dyspepsia, to borrow from Plum Wodehouse.

Muthu and I stood in his box in the members' stand.

'Well?'

I checked the betting cards. 'Three at 30 to one, two at 25 to one, three at 20 to one and two at 15 to one. That makes it one hundred and fifteen thousand rupees. And my four hundred at 30 to one—twelve thousand bucks. God, my hands are shaking.'

'They'll shake a lot more when you collect the money.'

'You're that confident?'

'Yes, we'll collect two and a half lakh rupees in another 10 minutes.'

The trumpet flourish which, in the Bangalore race course signals that the horses are being led to the starting gate, blasted out of the loudspeakers.

'Horses are now being stalled.' There were only eight runners and they were boxed quickly.

'And they are off.' Four words. Of one syllable each. Four syllables only. But they were a verbal fuse that set off a psychic explosion as twenty thousand pairs of eyes bored into eight horses and eight jockeys, as twenty thousand heartbeats speeded up, as twenty thousand minds hoped and prayed. I seemed to feel a stronger, almost palpable, force field around the two of us. The apparent boredom in the commentator's droning voice did nothing to lessen the tension. Indeed, the antithesis set off a bizarre contrast which made the predatory hysteria around and inside all the more frenzied.

'As they settle down, it is Chimera to the front, closely followed by Titan, a length away Simon Templar and Orace together, two lengths away Foundation, The Mule and Hari Selden in a close and two lengths away, the last is Centaur.'

I tore my eyes away from the horses and looked at Muthu. His face was obscured by a pair of binoculars; his hands were steady and his mouth relaxed. He must have felt my powerfully anxious gaze on him for, without taking away the binoculars, he said in a clear controlled voice: 'It's a mile race. Centaur will lie dead-last till the bend. Watch the fun in the last three hundred metres.'

Centaur's colours were all red with a black cap and it was easy to follow him even without binoculars. But as the horses neared the home turn, I lost him in the bunch.

'Nearing the home stretch, it is Chimera and Simon Templar together, a length away Orace and The Mule, a further length away Foundation, Centaur and Hari Selden. Titan is dropping back.'

Simon Templar was the favourite at even money and The Mule second favourite at two and a half to one.

'Entering the home stretch, it is Chimera, Simon Templar, The Mule, Foundation and Centaur. The rest are well behind.'

'Simon Templar has gone ahead now. (A roar from the crowd.). It is Simon Templar, The Mule, Centaur. Simon Templar and The Mule are together. (Another roar but much less powerful). Centaur is two lengths behind and the rest are out of the race.'

The horses were nearing the three hundred metre mark, with Simon Templar on the rails and The Mule alongside, but towards the centre of the race track, so that there was a gap of a couple of meters between them. Centaur was still a couple of lengths away but the jockey was not whipping him. It looked as if the race was between Simon Templar and The Mule.

The commentator apparently thought so too. It was difficult to hear him, the shouting of the crowd was almost deafening. Before the animal roar drowned him out, I heard the commentator, still droning, 'It's Simon Templar and The Mule. Both are going all out.'

Two hundred and fifty metres from home. Everyone had eyes for nothing but the two horses in front. But Muthu, who had dropped his binoculars, and I were watching Centaur.

And then it happened. Centaur burst forward. The jockey, Rixon, an Englishman pushing 55, had his whip in his left hand and was pushing with his right. The left hand was a blur, moving in a fast, rhythmical forwards and backwards action. On the forward stroke, the whip hit the horse under the next; the backward stroke slashed the rump. And the hand, not moving more than a few inches each time, all the power coming from the wrist, stabbed back and forth as the jockey crouched over his mount.

Two hundred metres from home, Centaur shot into the gap between Simon Templar and The Mule and drew level. Now, the three of them were fighting it out, nostrils flared, froth streaming from the jaws, every muscle and sinew putting in a supreme effort as the jockeys whipped and pushed and heeled them.

I found myself shouting 'Ken-taur, Ken-taur' (exposing my classical education) in a continuous chant that matched the ferocity and lust for the kill of the Australian crowds baying 'Lil-lee, Lil-lee, Lil-lee'.

The horses flashed past the winning post, seemingly in a three-horse dead-heat. I looked wildly at Muthu. He was lighting a cigarette and I fancied his hands trembled slightly. He took a deep puff, exhaled slowly through the nostrils, turned and smiled.

'Centaur has won by the shortest of short-heads. In fact, by a nose. We have won. And Bharat, how many times have I told you not to shout in the race course. It is not elegant.'

The roar had become a muted buzz. And then, dead silence as the announcer's voice broke out through the loudspeaker system.

'Your attention please. The judges have called for a photo to decide the winner. The horses involved in the photo-finish are horse number one Simon Templar, horse number four The Mule and horse number eight Centaur. Horse number seven Orace is place fourth.'

Excited chatter broke out. 'I tell you it is a three-horse dead-heat ... Simon Templar has won ... It's The Mule .... The bastards, it was a coup with Centaur .... What a race .... I'll never forget today .... All races are fixed .... If Centaur wins, I'll never step into a race course again ....'

Smiling broadly, Muthu offered me a packet of cigarettes. Benson and Hedges. Charminar is my brand, I can't afford anything else. I took one. I lit up and we took deep, contented puffs, letting the smoke trickle out, floating on victory and—there's only one word for it, charming outdated slang of the forties—boodle. I mentally saluted the *Indian Herald*'s minor prophet. But still, there was that shadow of doubt.

Which was dispelled by the announcer: 'Here are the results of the photo-finish.' A nerve shattering pause, unintentional certainly, but worthy of Hitchcock.

'Horse number eight, Centaur, first. Horse number one, Simon Templar, second. Horse number four, The Mule, third.'

Dead silence. On the lawns of the first enclosure on our right a group of five was celebrating, slapping each other's backs, shaking hands, laughing and shouting. The outsider-chasers. One of my friends is like that. He says that you go to the racecourse to gamble, to make quick, big and easy money; so you must back only outsiders. If you want a steady income and back the favourites, you might as well slog ten hours a day and make an honest living, he says.

Even then Muthu and I did not shake hands. There could be an objection. Then came the announcement, by a man with a BBC accent who spoke as if he had a hot, baked potato in his mouth: 'The white cone has been hoisted.' This meant that the result was finally official, that the other jockeys were not disputing it.

We had won. Muthu's take that day was two and a half lakhs. Mine was twelve thousand, more than a month's salary. We shook hands.

'Okay,' said Mr Hekyll 'It is our turn to draw the moral of the story.'

'Ladeees and gentulmain!' Mr Jyde waited for the imaginary drum roll of the circus orchestra to die down into a soft, thrumming murmur. 'The moral of the story is... ' He waited as the drum roll went into a crescendo and slowly died out once again.

'Ladeees and gentulmain, a horse normally covers 200 metres in fourteen seconds. In those last fourteen seconds of the race, a whole lifetime of high adventure, intolerable tension, emotional upheaval, pain, happiness and even lust had been encapsulated and popped into our good friend, Mr Bharat Sharma's mouth, like a superfast-acting virility pill. Life could hold nothing more exciting, intense, terrifying, glorious and deliriously, almost orgasmically, happy than those fourteen seconds. The rest of life would be an anti-climax. Happiness is not for ever after. It does not last more than fourteen seconds.'

'Right, Bharat?'

'Right, Mr Jyde.'

'Wrong, Bharat,' said Dr Hekyll. 'Happiness is both a process and an event. Bharat felt it for fourteen seconds. And it was like an emotional pill bomb popped into his mouth. But happiness can also bottled, like a perfume and sniffed whenever you are low. That's the trick to conquer unhappiness.'

# Chapter 10

*'Things fall apart; the Centre cannot hold'*

—The Second Coming W B Yeats

Whatever, you might say, Dr Hekyll and Mr Jyde, I am convinced the fairy tales have got it all wrong (I said).

Nobody lives happily ever after. I'll bet that five years after Prince Charming kissed her awake, Princess Aurora longed to prick her finger on the spindle and go back to sleep for another century.

Presidency College was happy to have me back. I had been one of the champion stallions of their stable and they had been sorry to see me go. But the sharpness was gone, the old fire had almost died out, only a few coals glowed dimly. I tried to stoke up the flames again, blowing and puffing hard in determination and desperation, but it was no use.

I could not immerse myself again in the glory of teaching. Brilliant students still came to my classes but I could not get involved with them, could not make the effort to peer into their minds and learn and understand and mold. I stuck it out for a few years but finally decided that I had better get out. I resigned and this time the college was not sorry to see me go, though I could see the silent pity welling out of the eyes of some of my colleagues.

I did nothing for six months, living off my savings. One day, I found that my bank balance was down to fifty rupees. I needed a job. I found one in the 'situations vacant' columns of the newspaper: a clerk in a stevedoring company. The office was on the third floor of one of those dingy buildings on Linghi Chetty Street, in the oldest part of Madras called Georgetown. I had a desk in a corner of a windowless room and a single bulb burned night and day but I never had enough light to work by. But it did not bother me. In the darkness of my mind, light was lethiferous. I had become a zombie. The only thing I looked forward to every day was the coming of night, spent in a booze-drenched carus brought on by three glasses of neat arrack. This went on for two years.

By that time, my divorce had come through. Renu had filed on grounds of desertion. I made a half-hearted attempt to get custody of the children, or at least one of them, but I never had a chance. The judge took one look at my bank pass book and another at Kailasam's bank's balance sheet and ruled that I could visit the children on Sunday afternoons for three hours and that they could spend a week with me every two years. I never went to visit the children and never asked them to spend a week with me. All ties were cut.

One day, I was bent over a ledger in the office when I heard someone walking towards my desk. I did not look up.

'You poor bastard', I heard a man say. I looked up and there was Muthu. He had some business with the company and had spotted me. Without saying another word, he pulled me upright and pushed me out of the room and that office. I went meekly.

Muthu knew Pahadia well and fixed me up as an apprentice reporter. I was 40 years old and I was paid a stipend of a thousand rupees.

Excerpts from

'Le Cahiers du Bharat Sharma'

## Prometheus

*I thought I saw an eagle swoop*
*But it was a vulture, tearing*
*At my jejunum.*
*Why my jejunum?*
*Why not my liver, or kidney?*
*Why say nix to my appendix?*
*There is no accounting for taste.*
*De gustibus, as grandpa used to say,*
*Non est disputandum.*

# INTERLUDE

He was walking along a narrow path in the hills, a two-foot-wide track of winding earth, thick with grass because few had used it in recent times. The path bored through a tunnel of trees, the topmost branches of which leaned towards each other, met and interlaced. The light, already dimmed by massive black clouds, grew dimmer as Shiva strode deeper into the forest. The flashes of lightning that crackled at the dry brown hills briefly lit up the path, so powerful they could pierce the thick blanket of branches and leaves. Thunder exploded like a grenade but inside the tunnel the sound was a muted thump.

'Darkness at Noon', Shiva thought. Arthur Koestler. A fine writer but he could not face the ultimate pain. Which man of vision, of clarity of purpose, would be weak enough to commit suicide? Koestler had thought he was attacking Communism but what he had written would apply equally to fascism, military dictatorships or even democracy.

Chanakya, Machiavelli, Lenin, Mao, Hobbes, Plato—they had all said it before. The King, the Prince, the Chairman, the General Secretary, the Prime Minister, all had to be strong, ruthless, if enlightened visions of few were to become the reality of billions.

The billions must be taught, moved, cajoled, pushed, tricked, bribed and bullied into wanting the change. The few who try will be resisted, hunted, tortured, killed and imprisoned. I am of the few. But I will prevail.

Another flash of lightning, drum rolls of thunder and the rain cascaded down. The thirsty hills gratefully sucked in the torrent. Within the canopy of trees, the rain fell in gentle drops, the flood filtered by the interlaced branches. Siva hitched the knapsack higher on his back and strode along. Soon, the forest thinned and the rain fell in a steady downpour. The path became steeper and Siva could feel the gradient by the pull on his calf muscles. But his breathing remained the same, strong and steady, the rise and fall of his chest barely visible. He was a superb specimen of young, male muscle and flesh and could keep up a grueling lope for hours on end. This was, for him, like an evening stroll.

The tree line ended. Shiva stopped to brush back his longish hair that had got plastered to his forehead, some strands falling across his eyes. Ahead of him, the mountain was sparsely vegetated, rocky, with a few stunted shrubs. The path twisted and writhed upwards. The crest of the hill he was climbing was a few hundred yards away.

A quick shiver passed through Shiva as a keen wind came slicing down from above and to the left. The rain fell at an angle now and another shiver passed through him.

He was at a height of about 7,500 feet above sea level and even in summer the Kodaikanal Hills could get cold.

Once again, Shiva settled the pack more comfortably on his shoulders and surged upwards. Five minutes later, he reached the top of the climb and reached a plateau which stretched for half mile, before the mountain range climbed skywards again. A couple of hundred yards ahead, a deep, thickly wooded ravine slashed into the bowels of the mountain.

'This is it,' Shiva thought, a tiny ball of excitement forming above his diaphragm.

He walked forward slowly till he was at the lip of the ravine, ten feet wide and broadening as it grew, looking like a lion's mane as seen by a mouse sitting on its back. At the edge of the ravine, on the left, was the landmark he had been told to look out for, a stunted tree growing out of a split rock. The path into the ravine was barely identifiable by flattened grass and disturbed leaves. Shiva walked on.

A minute later he was flat on his back, a thickly muscled forearm pressing hard into his throat as a knife glinted before his eyes.

'Who are you?'

Shiva was impressed. He answered in Hindi, as he had been instructed. 'My name is Shiva. I bring greetings from Charu. He wanted to know who would cook him fish curry, now that you are here.'

'Okay, it's him. Let him get up,' said another voice from behind him. The knife was removed and the pressure on Shiva's throat eased. He stood up and brushed the leaves and grass from his clothes. Two young men stood in front of him. The taller of the two, still holding the knife, grinned and put out his hand.

'Welcome, comrade. I am Srihari. This is Ramesh. We have been looking forward to meeting you. Come, let us go to the camp. Lunch should be ready, it's a special one in your honour and I am hungry enough to eat a buffalo.'

* * *

The three young men talked late into the night, pulling down the Universe and rebuilding it, smashing to pieces what they rebuilt and reconstructing again. The fire around which they sat leaped and roared and danced like their imagination and their phenomenology of the past, the present and the future.

Ramesh was the fiery one; ideas and words spat out rat-a-tat, like the AK 47 with which he would mow down class enemies, ideological bullets that ricocheted off the cold and dark mountains. 'Annihilation', his very soul thundered. 'Destroy, wipe out, rebuild, remold.'

Srihari was quieter, but he too rumbled with menace, a bubbling pressure cooker ready to blast off scalding steam, but prevented by the weight of the tactical and strategic weaknesses of the little group. 'Annihilate, yes; but the time is not ripe.'

Shiva sat, listened, ingested, thought: 'Force is the only tool to wrench out entrenched forces. The history of Man proves this thesis. The antithesis is the proposition that an object will remain in its position of rest or motion along a straight line unless acted upon by a more powerful force. The scientific knowledge of Mankind proves this. The synthesis? Wait till you are strong enough, to exert the necessary force without risking annihilation yourself. Death, yes. That comes to all men. But self-immolation? No.'

Ramesh glared at Srihari and shouted: 'The time is not ripe. The time is not ripe. The time is not ripe. That's what we have been saying for decades, sitting on our butts in cozy armchairs. Now. Now is the time to act. We must act now. We haven't the time to wait.'

'And get out butts and brains shot off and put back the revolution by another century?' growled Srihari. 'No, comrade, no. What happened in Srikakulam? What happened in Naxalbari? What happened in Calcutta? What is happening in Andhra?'

Ramesh jumped up and vented his anger on an overhanging branch. He wrenched it off the tree and tore away the leaves. He viciously broke up the branch and threw the bits into the fire.

Shiva spoke, almost dreamily: 'Comrades, both of you know what must be done. But you are allowing your emotions to control your thinking. In your minds you know that we have to gather strength quickly. We can't act now. But we can't wait long either. The first requirement is to get enough strength to apply irresistible force. How do we grow strong enough? Guns, bullets, money. Yes, these are necessary. But the essential condition is a solid mass base. Do we, not just our group but all committed comrades put together, have this kind of strength? No. We all agree with Srihari on that fact. Also, we all agree with Ramesh that we have done nothing to make ourselves strong. I agree that we have reclined in armchairs, or relaxed around campfires, talking all the while.

'So, what do we do now? The theory is known. Go out to the peasantry. Win them over to our side. Become their friend. Become a part of them. Push them, teach them, prod them, cajole them, force them to rise and demand and fight. But not just with words. With action. Not just by leading agitations, though this is necessary. We have to prove to the peasantry, the landless labourers that we can protect them from retaliation when they bestir themselves. To do that, we need to kill the oppressor. We need to kill selectively, since we are not powerful enough. The brutal policeman, the lecherous landlord, the exploitative businessman, the corrupt politician and the extortionist trader. It has to be an advance on all fronts, our base rooted firmly in the soil and those who till it.'

Silence fell. The fire leaped and crackled. The three young men dreamt on, pulling down the unresponding Universe, rebuilding it, smashing to pieces what they had built and reconstructing again.

* * *

The three young men came to the village in the plains when the sun was at its zenith, burning up an already burnt land. An old man squatted by the side of the little road, waiting for nothing, not even God. He was not really an old man, nor was the road really a road. It was a ten-foot-wide dirt track, so dry that even the ruts made by bullock cart wheels were dusty. There had been no rain for three years and the track was as desiccated as the old man, who was in his late forties but looked to be seventy years old.

Aeons ago, he had squatted in the same way at the same spot, looking heavenwards for cloud-sign. He had waited for the rain that had never come. He had waited for the landlord's men who had come and demanded his crop, though little had grown and bellies in the village had shrunk closer to backbones. The old man had squatted and watched while the landlord's men took away goats and chickens and pigs and cattle, when they found there was no grain.

Now, the old man squatted and waited for nothing; but his eyes were alive, the only moving parts of his body, watching with endless and eternal patience the antics of a sparrow that hopped on the roadside, a lizard that slithered between rocks filmed with dust. Occasionally his eyes flicked leftwards towards the highway a couple of kilometers away. This was where an infrequent bus or truck laboured past and rightwards to the village a few hundred yards away, where the cry of a mother calling to her child hung still in the dry, burning air.

He was watching a snail crawling near his ankle when Shiva came to a halt a few feet away, dropped the two heavy canvas bags he was carrying on the road, folded his hands and said: 'Vanakkam, Ayya.'

Moving his head as slowly as the snail he was observing so intently, the old man looked up at the three young men. His eyes had gone completely blank, dull pebbles that had once shone brightly at the swaying hips of the singing women of the village as they brought water home from the river, pots delicately balanced on their heads. He stared silently.

'Vanakkam, Ayya,' Shiva said again.

The old man nodded in greeting and stood up slowly, inborn courtesy winning over wariness and apathy. There was something peculiar about these young men. They were dressed in dhoties and khaki cotton shirts and looked like city people, but the villager felt a strange affinity with them. They had that stillness at the centre which the old man had often found in himself and rarely saw in the men and women who came from the cities. These city dwellers came to lift the rural masses out of the mire and taught them basket weaving and the theory of the co-operative movement. These men and women came to soothe their egos and feed their appetites for movement without action. In contrast, these young men exuded a deadly calm, a hidden sense of menacing purpose that excited and frightened the old man.

Shiva introduced them. They were from Madras, he explained, and were skilled in repairing cycles, water pumps, anything that needed to be set right. The city had suffocated them. Anyway, they had been unable to find jobs. So they had come to the village with the hope of putting up a small foundry and a repair shop to make a living. All their tools and accessories were in the canvas bags they carried, Shiva said. Could the old man tell them whom they should meet so that they could find a room to set up shop and another to live in?

Why did they come to this village?

Oh, they just took a map and stuck a pin in it, Shiva laughed.

The old man nodded. The young men were lying, of course. They had a more deadly purpose in coming here. But then, the old man did not mind. It would be a change from waiting for nothing. Come with me, he said, and led the way into the village.

* * *

It is easy to kill, Shiva thought without surprise as the knife slipped through the ribs, angled upwards and tore open the heart. Sometimes in the past, he had wondered what it would feel like being the agent of death who metamorphoses a living, dreaming, rutting, philosophising human organism into a mass of dead, stiff and stinking flesh. Would he feel godlike, omnipotent, orgasmic? Or would he slide into a guilt-ridden depressive psychosis? These thoughts had never occupied his mind for long. He had not brushed them aside; they had slid away naturally, like the mild glandular stirrings of the teenager as he watches the woman next door combing her hair at the window.

Now he had done it, executed his first kill—or murder or assassination or execution—it all depended on how you looked at it. The twisting knife stopped the man's heart in its rhythmic pumping. The pot-bellied ex-convict—once charged with the murder of a Harijan family, but allowed by the courts to go free because eyewitnesses had been frightened into silence—who stood guard at the landlord's two-storied mansion in Kanakapurm, died with a gurgling moan that could not be heard ten paces away.

The stout staff the dead man had been carrying slipped from his hand and Shiva grabbed at it, so that it would not clatter on the stone steps leading up to the gate and alert the house. Irulandi, the landless labourer who was Shiva's first 'convert', began his baptism by catching the guard under the arms and easing the body soundlessly to the ground.

Irulandi pulled out the bunch of heavy keys tucked into the guard's dhoti at the waist and started trying each key in the massive lock on the gate. The fifth one clicked. Irulandi slipped the lock off and drew the bolt with infinite care. Still, there was a faint screech as the rusty bolt came free and Shiva and Irulandi froze.

A dog barked in the distance but there was no sound of human beings awakening. Irulandi opened the gate wide enough for a man to pass through and Shiva whistled softly. A dozen shadows darted across the dusty street and filed silently into the courtyard of the landlord's house.

The last was a girl, not yet twenty years old, black as the night in which they moved stealthily, short, thin, large liquid eyes dominating a bony, haggard face. As she neared Shiva who stood near the gate, she stopped, bent down and touched his feet.

'Thank you, elder brother. That monster inside raped and murdered my younger sister. She was only fourteen. He sent my father to prison and broke my mother's mind. He dies. He dies now. He dies as horribly as my sister died. No, don't come in. Go away. That man is our prey. We will do it. It is our duty. It is our revenge.'

Shiva touched her lightly on the head and walked away.

Shiva thought: 'The seed I planted has grown into a shrub. It is a cactus that will tear and cut and mangle the hands that try to pull it out by the roots. It will grow and multiply in the stony desert in which I walk. I will slake the thirst of those who follow me.'

* * *

Shiva checked into the luxurious penthouse suite of the Majestic Hotel in Madras. He was dressed casually in a light grey safari suit but one look at his handmade shoes of soft leather, the slim gold watch on his left wrist, the fragile looking sunglasses pushed up above his forehead and the custom-made Italian leather suitcase, told even the casual observer that this was Mr Moneybags, only son of Daddy Warbucks.

In the suite, the bellboy gently deposited the suitcase in a wardrobe half the size of a one-room tenement in a Bombay chawl and saluted smartly. Shiva casually tossed a hundred rupee note in his direction and ambled to the window to look down at the city, the sky over which was turning a dirty pink, as the sun slipped quickly down the western horizon. As the bellboy backed out of the room murmuring awed gratitude, Shiva called room service and ordered a bottle of Royal Salute Scotch whisky and grilled tiger prawns. He hated alcohol and prawns gave him a pain in the tummy, but he had to play every role he set for himself to perfection. He had to; it was literally a matter of life and death if he deviated even minutely from the characteristic behaviour of the person he was pretending to be at any time.

The whisky and the prawns arrived. Soon after came Goverdandas Shah, who owned one of the city's biggest stock broking companies and whose services Shiva had used since the age of eighteen, when he was given control of the trust fund his grandfather had set up the day he was born. The ten lakh rupees that had formed the original corpus had grown fifteen times when he had taken charge. By the time he had finished college, Shiva had trebled his assets through trading on the stock exchange and on the bullion and commodity markets. He was indeed the grandson of his grandfather and the son of his mother. He had financed most of the arms deals from his own funds. And he kept making more money from the markets, using Shah as his only conduit.

Shah had been a stockbroker for nearly 50 years and knew everything there was to know about converting profits into black money. Since he was totally without any moral sense, he did not care what Shiva did with the money, though he knew what was going on. He was also bound to Shiva with hoops of steel because Shiva's grandfather had helped him in the early days. He was totally loyal to Shiva. Of course, he charged a considerable fee for whatever he did. That was one thing about which he could never compromise.

A tall, thin old man, Shah was dressed in what could be described as his working uniform: dhoti tied in the traditional style with one end looped between the legs and tucked in at the waist, a long black 'bandgala' coat coming down to his knees and a khadi 'Nehru' cap. He was brisk and wasted little time. A curt 'namaste' and he opened the small suitcase he had been carrying. It was stacked full of five hundred rupee notes.

'Fifty lakhs here. And thirty lakhs will be delivered at the indicated place at ten o'clock in the morning to the person you have nominated.'

Shiva glanced briefly at the suitcase, flipped it closed and tossed it on the bed. For fifteen minutes they discussed future investments. Shiva decided to keep out of the stock markets for the next four months; there were few indications about which way they would move. Shah agreed that this was a sound strategy. He suggested forward purchases in groundnuts and gold. Shiva did some quick mental calculations and instructed Shah to put fifty lakhs in gold and twenty lakhs in groundnuts. Shah left soon after, assuring Shiva that he was always at his service.

At nine o'clock, there was a soft knock on the door. A handsome middle aged man dressed in a three piece suit came in. Shiva poured him a drink and they waited in silence. Ten minutes later the phone rang. Shiva picked it up. It was Srihari. 'My daughter arrived on the flight from Trivandrum. She would like to see you and pay her respects.' This was the signal that a consignment of arms had been delivered. 'Fine, I'll meet her in the morning,' Shiva said and put the phone down. He handed the briefcase to the arms dealer. The man had another quick drink and left.

* * *

'You know who that young man is, of course,' said Dr Hekyll. Mr Jyde nodded agreement.

I knew who he was. He was my son, Lakshman, who changed his name to Shiva after he became a Naxalite. The financial wizard with a social conscience. Social conscience? He was a warrior in this age when little men lived by what little wits their undersized brains contained.

'Yes, Bharat,' said Dr Hekyll and Mr Jyde together. 'He's a warrior. You are proud of him.'

# Part II

# The Conquest of Happiness

# Chapter 11

*'Some days are born ugly....Oh, it's awful on such a day. The postman brings overdue bills.'*

—'Sweet Thursday', John Steinbeck

'Okay, Bharat,' said Dr Hekyll, 'from now on we will not interrupt you. Only if you go through the next few chapters of your past life by yourself, will the cathartic process work. Therefore, Mr Jyde, no more fatuous remarks from you till I say so.'

'Don't pontificate. I know what must be done,' growled Mr Jyde. 'My remarks are always to the point, I am never fatuous.'

'What nonsense, I never pontificate.' Dr Hekyll prepared to move away into his retreat in my basal ganglia.

I stepped in: 'Shut up, both of you. I need to concentrate on this.'

I got back home from work one day (I said) around six o'clock in the evening. I had a long, cold shower and put on a fresh dhoti and kurta. I had just poured myself a tall rum and water with lots of ice when there was a knock on the door.

I opened the door and there she was.

'What the hell,' I shouted. 'Renu! Renuka Bharat!. Or is it Renuka Kailasam again?'

She stood stiffly upright, her face cold, her head tilted back in arrogance, the ice maiden, now an ice matron.

'Age has not improved your manners, I see. Aren't you going to invite me in?' she asked.

'Age does not wither her nor custom stale her infinite malice. Come in. Sit down.'

I asked her to take the cane chair while I sat on the bed. She had not changed much in two decades: the same stupendous figure, bursting breasts, a still slim waist flowing into hips that had widened just a trace. Only the minute, almost invisible lines on her face showed that she was over forty.

'Well, well, Mohammed comes to the mountain,' I said with a twisted smile.

'There is no need to be flippant. You know very well I wouldn't have come except in an emergency. And, as you should well know, I wouldn't have come if the crisis involved only me. I don't need you to solve my personal problems. I have come because it involves our son, Lakshman, and you have a responsibility towards him.'

I laughed. I laughed long and hard; so long and hard that I could hear the rising note of hysteria.

'Shut up.' Her voice was like a whiplash. It rocked me back to normality.

'Our son!' I shouted. 'Our son? He was our son only for six years. After that, he has been your son. I don't know him. He is a stranger to me.'

She was unmoved, cold. 'He is our son because he was born to us. You and I made love and created him.'

'And what's he done?' I snarled. 'Knocked up the servant maid? Killed a slum child in a drunken driving accident? Does he snort cocaine? Is he mainlining on heroin? That's the kind of crisis a young man in your type of family needs to be pulled out of.'

'Stop trying to hurt me. You can't. You never had the power to hurt me. And that kind of thing is not a crisis. I can handle such things in my sleep. He's got into a different kind of mess. It wouldn't have happened if you weren't his father. I thought I was very clever when I hooked you, but I know now that it was the stupidest thing I have done in my life.'

'I haven't seen the boy for two decades and I'm responsible for whatever he's done? Come, Renu, even you can't be so blind.'

'Will you allow me to tell you what has happened? You can preach later.'

'Like a drink?' I asked as I freshened up my drink.

'I don't drink rum.' She wrinkled her nose as I lit a Charminar.

'Suit yourself. Now, tell me.'

'Lakshman has become a Naxalite.'

I was silent for a while. Then I spoke slowly, carefully spacing out the words, trying to hurt her, trying to twist the knife deep in her guts. 'That is the best news I have heard since the lawyers told me our divorce had gone through. I am glad the boy has not been ruined, after all.

I thought he would have become the perfect banker, with a calculator in his heart, red ink in his veins and a ledger for a brain.'

'Shut up,' she screamed, the iron control breaking down. 'He's going to die, you bastard, tortured and shot down like a mad dog and you have the infinite gall to sit there smugly and spout stinking rubbish!'

We sat in silence for a few minutes.

She sat back and composed herself. She looked a stone idol painted over with a thin film of pulchritudinous flesh. Her voice deepened; it came from somewhere in the tomb she had created around herself to hold in her grief and to prevent me from seeing how much she was hurting. In a tone with few inflections, like a poor actor reciting lines he can never understand, she intoned:

'I always wanted Lakshman to be the perfect banker. I trained him. I molded him to be just that. And he was going to be just that. He is brilliant. He was far and away the best student in the University. He got his master's degree in commerce. First class, first rank, the highest marks that anyone has got in the history of Madras University. I did not want him to study abroad. I wanted him to infuse into his soul a feel of how Indian businessmen think, feel, act, love and do business. Five firms of chartered accountants wanted to take him in. But he said he wanted to take six months off; to travel and see the real India. And then, another six months to prepare for the bank probationary officers' exam. I agreed. That was the blunder. But later it turned out that I had started losing control earlier. I did not know that he had been moving around with a leftist gang in his final year in college. He was close to a girl, a muddled twit named Shailaja, who filled his head with a load of nonsense about revolution and rousing the smelly masses to fight against injustice.

One day, about a year ago, he disappeared. He left a note for me, saying that he had decided on what he wanted to do in life and therefore he had become a Naxalite. I didn't give up. I tried to keep a watch on him. A very close friend is high up in the police. Through him I got bits and pieces of news about Lakshman. He calls himself Shiva now...'

I jumped up. 'What? Repeat that? Shiva? Why, the police are calling him the mastermind behind the Krishnapuri bomb blast and the Loganatha Mudaliar massacre. They are trying to pin other murders and dacoities on him.'

'Yes.' She had not moved, still hewn from granite, not melting. 'That monster is what Lakshman has become. And I blame you for it. The romantic streak he inherited from you drove him into this horror, this excrescence of an excuse for living. I've decided what must be done. We have to get him out. Force is the only way. He will not listen to reason. Maybe a couple of years from now, when the first flush of revolutionary passion fades, he may be willing to listen to intellectual arguments, that the way he has chosen to liberate his fellow men is bound to fail. But there isn't time. Any day now, the police will arrest him. He does not have the mass backing of a Mao Zedong or a Ho Chi Minh. His own followers may betray him soon. So we must get him out by force.'

'What do you mean?'

'He must be kidnapped, maybe drugged into unconsciousness or immobilised in some other way and taken out of the country. I have made all the arrangements. A smugglers' boat will, in a couple of weeks at the most, be ready to get him out of the country any time of the day or night. A hand-picked gang of goondas is ready to kidnap him. The smugglers will pick him up somewhere on the west coast, south of Bombay, and take him to Dubai. From there, he will be flown to Canada. I have already paid an advance of fifty lakh rupees and half a million dollars will be paid when he is safely in Canada. Now, we have to find him and grab him before the police do.'

'Did you work out this plan all by yourself?'

'I had some help.'

'Ah, that very close friend who is high up in the police?'

She hesitated. She turned her face away, for the first time since she had come into the house.

'Answer me!'

'Yes.'

'What's his name?

No answer.

'Are you lovers?'

Her head turned sharply back to me, anger and menace in her eyes. 'That is immaterial to the present discussion.'

'You have to tell me who he is and what is the relationship between the two of you. Otherwise, I will not help you.'

'Have I asked for your help?'

'Don't fool around with me Renuka. You did not come here and disclose your dangerous plan just because I am his father and you felt a wifely duty to keep me informed. We are strangers now. You want me to help in some way. And I will not help unless I know which policeman is helping you. I must be convinced that, after I help and Shiva gets away ...'

She screamed: 'Don't call him by that obscene name. He is Lakshman, do you hear. Lakshman.'

'I can think of him only as Shiva. But, let's leave that aside. I must be convinced that after he gets away, your policeman friend does not make me a scapegoat and pin his escape on me. They could lock me up and throw away the key. I would be surprised if this is not already part of your plans. So, I must know his name. You don't have to answer the other question because I can guess the answer. You are lovers but you are not in love with him. You are using him.'

Renuka shouted: 'All right, shut up. His name is Gopalan.'

'The police commissioner! But I shouldn't really be surprised. And what do you want me to do? Not that I have agreed to help you.'

Renuka became brisk and businesslike. She sensed she had won. 'It may be necessary to hide Lakshman in Madras for a few days to throw the police off the track. Your house is the last place they will think of looking. They will trace him back to me but not to you. Except for Gopalan, nobody knows that you are his father. I have made sure of that at least, these past two decades and more. They may finally find the connection between the two of you but by then it will be too late. By then, he will be out of the country. Will you do it? Will you help your son?'

I stood up, walked to the table and poured myself another drink. I took a few short sips and went back to my chair.

'I don't know. I don't know whether I owe anything to anybody. He is a stranger to me.'

She smiled; a cold, grim smile. 'What's he to Hecuba or Hecuba to him?'

'You're quoting Hamlet out of context. The correct quotation is

*What's Hecuba to him, or he to Hecuba,*

*That he should weep for her? What would he do,*
*Had he the motive and the cue for passion*
*That I have?*

Renuka smiled again. 'Thank you, Dr Bharat Sharma.'

'Shut up, Renu. I need time. I need time to think about it. And there's another factor that you have ignored, that you could not have considered, given the way your mind thinks and your soul functions.'

'And what's that?'

'Your plan is bound to fail. Not because you are inefficient, but because you are trying to play God. You are trying to use force to bend Shiva's will to your own. Nobody has the right to do that to any human being. And anybody who tries to do that will surely fail.'

Renuka stood up. 'Spare me your philosophy. Don't think too long. Decide soon. I'll send a man tomorrow night. Just tell him yes or no. Don't say anything more to him.'

She opened the door. She stepped out and turned to face me.

'I know what your answer will be.' The words were a sneer. 'You are a romantic.'

* * *

The next day, I started my own hunt for my son. I found out that the 'muddled twit called Shailaja' was the daughter of a journalist acquaintance of mine. The recommendation of the father helped allay Shailaja's suspicions about my being a muck-raking journalist who only wanted to betray Lakshman. I convinced her that I was Lakshman's father and had not seen him for more than twenty years.

Lakshman and Shailaja had met in college and, like most intelligent young people of that generation, had walked gingerly along the streams of socialism, sometimes dipping their toes in the water. Their first major foray into activism came when some the news broke that the police had gunned down three suspected Naxalites, who had holed up in a village near Tirupattur.

A human rights group had quickly formed an 'enquiry committee' to probe deeply into the incident and come out with a report that was to be publicised all over the country. The committee was headed by Michael Raj, professor of history in Madras University. Lakshman and Shailaja volunteered and were joined by one other man and woman, Erwin Menezes from Goa and Urmila from Hyderabad.

I coaxed the full story of what happened to the enquiry committee from Shailaja.

Our first stop was at Kiliyanur (Shailaja said), where Professor Michael knew some workers of the Communist Party of India. There were only two of them in the local party office. They told us that a dozen of their comrades had been arrested, along with some civil rights activists, only that morning on charges of aiding and abetting Naxalite dacoits. It seemed that two nights previously a gang had forcibly entered the house of a big landlord in a village fifteen miles away and had robbed him of gold, jewellery and thirty thousand rupees. The landlord and his henchmen had been mercilessly beaten up and his wife and children had been tied up. The police found Naxalite slogans like 'Death to class enemies' and 'Annihilation is the first step to revolution' daubed in red paint on the walls. The Communist party cadres in Kiliyanur told us that it was the work of a gang of dacoits which had been operating in the area for some months. There had been other robberies and murders before and in each case Naxalite slogans and pamphlets had been found. The dacoits, they said, were deliberately throwing the blame on Naxalites in the area who did not subscribe to the annihilation line. They said that the police might themselves have painted the slogans and hinted that many cops were in league with the dacoits, sharing the booty.

We asked them to give us a guide to take us to some of the villages where Naxalites were active and to villages which had suffered from police repression. They said no one would come, all were terrified. They could not come with us because they had to get their comrades out on bail. So we decided to drive on to Ratnapuram to meet Mr Santhanam and try and get some help from him. On the way, Lakshman suggested that we drive into one of the villages just off the main road and try our luck. So we turned into the first dirt road leading to a village. It was a good thing we did, since we got first-hand experience of the fear that stalked the land there.

As soon as our car entered the main street of the village, the people scattered, shouting, 'Run, the police are here.' The men ducked into alleys and ran off into the fields while women snatched babies and herded children into their houses and bolted the doors. Within seconds there were hardly a dozen people in sight. Half of them were sitting on benches outside a tea-shop. We got out of the car and walked up to them. From inside the car, Lakshman had been clicking photographs of the fleeing men, women and children. We approached an old man sipping tea. 'Vanakkam, Ayya', said Professor Michael. The man did not respond, staring into his glass of tea. The Professor explained who we were and introduced all of us in turn. The old man thawed enough to raise his folded hands in greeting. We ordered tea and sat on the benches. No one spoke to us. A young boy, dressed only in a pair of torn shorts, his little buttocks open to the wind and sun, served us. There was none of the intense curiosity and generous hospitality that pervades a village in India when strangers arrive.

Lakshman broached the subject of Naxalites and police harassment. The men glanced nervously at each other and kept silent. I pressed them further. They answered sullenly, not looking us in the face, heads bent, staring at the hard-baked mud floor of the tea shop. 'The village was peaceful. Policemen rarely came here. Actually the arrests and beatings had taken place in the next village. This was a Harijan village and they were left alone.'

We knew we could get nothing from them but frightened lies. We left and went on to Ratnapuram which is a fairly big town, the taluk headquarters. We drove straight to Mr Santhanam's house. He was away at the court but was expected back in half-an-hour. His clerk welcomed us warmly and gave us coffee and sticky sweets. He then introduced us to two young men who were also waiting for Mr Santhanam. They were lecturers in the local college but they lived with their families in a village a few miles away from town. They told us that the police had rounded up ten landless labourers in the village for 'questioning'. This was a couple of days previously and the men had not returned. The two young men wanted Mr Santhanam to find out what had happened to the labourers. As we were chatting, Mr Santhanam came in.

Professor Michael, who is an old friend of Mr Santhanam, introduced all of us. Lakshman and Urmila took out tape recorders, remarking that they would not switch them on if Mr Santhanam had any objections. 'Go ahead', Santhanam said. Professor Michael then made a formal statement outlining the purpose of the visit and noting that the interview took place at such-and-such a time on such-and-such day. Before we could continue, the driver of the tourist taxi came in and said two policemen had questioned him about who we were and why we had come to see Mr Santhanam. They asked for our names but the taxi driver said he did not know anything. The driver was worried and said that if we were going to get involved with the police, he would have no alternative but to leave us and go back to Madras. Mr Santhanam and Professor Michael assured him that nothing would happen to him. The driver did not look convinced and so Lakshman gave him a hundred-rupee note and told him to go and have his lunch. The man went away looking less unhappy.

We talked to Mr Santhanam for a couple of hours. We've got it all down in our report. I'll give you just the gist of what he said. According to him, landless labourers and small tenant farmers had been restive for some time mainly because the continuing drought of the previous few years had pushed their earnings below subsistence level. North Arcot and Dharmapuri have rocky soil in most places and, at the best of times, agriculture is not a paying proposition. But the big landlords who, by their political clout got around the land ceiling laws, refused to bring down rents or increase wages. In desperation some landless labourers and small farmers started demanding more. They were ruthlessly crushed, the men beaten up by hired toughs, cottages and huts burned down, women molested and some even raped. The police were in the pay of the big landlords and actively aided the repression. A favourite technique was to arrest people indiscriminately on flimsy charges and then release them on bail. But the condition was that they had to report to the police station in Ratnapuram or Tirupattur every day. The men lived in faraway villages and had to make the trip to the towns every day. This meant that they could not work in the fields and could not earn their daily bread. The situation was ripe for the influx of leftist activists from outside who started organising the landless labourers and peasants to demand a decent living. This brought more repression and any activist who talked of a better deal for the poor was dubbed a Naxalite. There was even a man belonging to the DMK, the mainstream political party that had had several stints at ruling Tamil Nadu, who had been arrested on charges of being a Naxalite and a dacoit, Mr Santhanam told us. He said the frustration in the poorer people was building up to danger levels and predicted that one day there would be a mass explosion; the peasants would take up their sickles and scythes and lash out blindly at whoever stood in their way. That might have begun happening in the two districts now. It was happening all over India, but in pockets, in several States. There were thousands of Naxalbaris ready to erupt.

Mr Santhanam promised to arrange a guide to take us to a few villages, a local man who would inspire confidence in the people whom we wanted to interview. We arranged to pick up the guide at Mr Santhanam's house the next morning. We then went to the local magistrate's court but we were not allowed to look at any documents. They told us to talk to the Deputy Inspector-General who was based in Tirupattur or to the top brass in Madras. All the while, we were shadowed by two policemen in uniform. At one point, Lakshman challenged them and asked them why they were following us. He was told to mind his business. If he created any trouble, there was enough room in the cells in the police station, they warned us.

By that time, it was growing dark and we decided to find rooms for the night. There was only one hotel which looked clean enough and we got two adjoining rooms there, one for the men and one for the women, on the first floor. After we washed, we met in our room for a cup of coffee and a review of what we had gleaned during the day. As we were comparing notes, the manager of the hotel came in and said that according to the rules we had to enter the names and addresses of all five of us in the register. We had checked in as Prof Michael and party. This was something new to us, but we did not suspect anything immediately.

As Prof Michael was taking down our addresses, we heard a faint roar outside but we could not make out what was happening. The noise grew louder: it sounded like a mob of people shouting something and coming towards the hotel. Something made Lakshman lock the door of the room. Within minutes we could make out the sounds clearly and to our shock realised that the mob was shouting slogans against us. We rushed to the window and looked out. There were about a hundred people on the street at the entrance to the lodge. They were led by a man who was reading out slogans from a piece of paper in his hand. Another shock ran through us as we recognised him as the policemen who had been following us, the one Lakshman had challenged. He had changed into plain clothes. We could now clearly make out what they were shouting. The policemen shouted out a slogan and the mob repeated it: 'inquiry committee, go back; down with the Naxalites; Naxal lovers, your time has come; we want police protection.'

We could make out more policemen in plain clothes at the head of the crowd. Suddenly, ten tough-looking men broke away from the crowd and ran into the lodge. They rushed up the stairs and tried to break the door down but luckily it held. A few of them peered through the ventilators set near the ceiling and shouted obscenities at us, particularly at Urmila and me. I was dead scared and started whimpering. Lakshman put his arm around me and soothed me, saying nothing would happen, the mob would go away after a while, we would be safe. Then there was silence in the corridor and a lone voice called out: 'Professor Michael, I am Inspector Anbarasu. You met me at the police station. I have come to protect you. Please open the door and let me in. I want to talk to you. I assure you that no one else will get in.'

Prof Michael looked at us. 'No, no, no', said Urmila and Erwin together, but Lakshman said, ''We have to open the door if we are to get out of here safely. But we'll take precautions.' He picked up a rickety old chair and broke off the legs. Holding one in each hand, he stood next to the door. 'Open the door, Professor. If anyone else tries to get in, I'll knock him out.' The precautions proved unnecessary since only Inspector Anbarasu stood at the door; the rest had retreated to the end of the corridor at the head of the stairs. We quickly bolted the door after Anbarasu came in.

Prof Michael was in a towering rage. 'What is all this nonsense, Inspector? Here we are minding our own business and we are threatened by a mob and a police-inspired mob, it seems. I demand that you give us protection.'

Anbarasu bristled: 'Allegations like that will get you nowhere, mister; they'll land you in trouble. What do you mean, police-inspired mob? You sneaking snoops come here and make trouble, rouse the anger of the people by supporting these murdering Naxalites and you accuse us patriotic policemen of threatening you. Because of you, I have a law and order problem on my hands and I don't have enough personnel to control that mob outside if it turns violent. Why do you busybodies come here and try to create riots?'

Prof Michael was spluttering wordlessly in a near-apoplectic rage. Lakshman growled menacingly and moved towards Anbarasu, the chair legs raised. I pulled him back, while Urmila addressed Anbarasu: 'All that is neither here nor there, Inspector. How do you propose to protect us from that vicious mob, police-inspired or not?'

'Now you're talking sense, Madam,' said Anbarasu. 'I have pacified them somewhat. There is a police van waiting outside to take you out of town. Pack your bags and we'll leave in five minutes. I shall protect you, with this revolver, if necessary' .

Lakshman butted in: 'We can't do that. We can't leave now. Our work here is not finished yet.'

Scowling, Anbarasu told Lakshman, 'You had better finish your work here in five minutes, mister, or the mob out there will finish you. I can't keep those angry people outside under control for long.'

'How do we know this is not a trap? How do we know you are not luring us outside with false promises only to throw us to that mob? After all, one of your subordinates was reading out the slogans out there,' asked Urmila.

'Madam,' said Anbarasu, 'look out of the window and you will see the van standing on the road. And if you can't trust a policeman, whom can you trust?'

'That's the best joke I've heard in years', Lakshman said as he moved to the window. 'Yes, there is a van in the street but it is at least 15 feet away from the lodge entrance. Can't you get it nearer? There are 50 people between the van and the entrance.'

'That's the best I can do. Be ready to leave in five minutes', Anbarasu said and went out.

We packed quickly. The men got their bags from their room and came back. My hands were shaking. Lakshman took my hands in his and squeezed gently and smiled. I felt better. The mob outside started roaring again. Anbarasu knocked on the door and shouted, 'Come out, it's safe.'

Lakshman led the way out, followed by the Professor and the two of us girls. Erwin brought up the rear. A dozen toughs were still standing at the head of the stairs. As they saw us, they started shouting 'Death to the Naxalites, Inquiry Committee down, down.'

They moved slowly backwards as Anbarasu advanced, shooing them back. We moved forward warily. We were half-way down the stairs and the goondas and Anbarasu were in the lobby on the ground floor, when one of them let loose a stone at us. It missed Lakshman narrowly as he ducked. With a roar of rage, five of them shoved Anbarasu aside and charged up the stairs. We turned and ran back into our room. One of them caught up with Lakshman and tried to pull him back. Lakshman turned in one fluid movement and kicked the toughie in the balls. The man crumpled to the floor without a sound, his hands clutching his crotch. Lakshman was angry enough to charge the rest but we pulled him back and bolted the door. Once again, the goondas started hammering at the door and shouting obscene words at us. This went on for a few minutes and then we heard Anbarasu shouting 'Get back down the stairs, you idiots.'

There was silence and a few seconds later we heard sounds of the men walking back to the stairs. Anbarasu hammered on the door and shouted: 'Okay, it's safe to come out now.' Lakshman opened the door slightly and peered out: 'He's got his gun in his hand', he said. Anbarasu shouted again, 'Yes I've got my revolver out and will use it if necessary to protect you; though why I should fire on my own people, I don't know.' We looked at Professor Michael. He nodded silently and we trooped out. This time Anbarasu stayed close to us, waving his gun about and the toughs gave ground slowly. We walked down the stairs, through the lobby and into the street. The crowd parted before us. We took a few steps towards the police van and then all hell broke loose.

With a terrifying shout, the mob closed in around us. Filthy hands clutched at me, pawed me in obscene lust, tried to tear my sari and blouse away, pummelled me on the head and back and breasts. I felt a terrible pain as something struck my forehead, lights flashed in my eyes and I became half-unconscious. I dimly saw Lakshman fight his way back towards me; blood was pouring down his face which was contorted in uncontrollable rage. He kicked and clawed and punched his way towards me and lifted me up in his arms. Then two shots rang out. Anbarasu had fired in the air and all was silent. He could have done it when the mob first attacked but the bastard wanted us to be beaten up. He and a couple of policemen then pushed and dragged us towards the van. As we were getting in, the mob charged again and tried to drag us out. They caught hold of Erwin's legs but he kicked out and caught a man in the nose. I heard the sound of crunching bone and blood spurted out of the man's face as he screamed and fell. The van took off but the mob ran after us, screaming its rage and frustration. Once again, at the head of the chasing mob, I saw a policeman in plain clothes.

We were taken to Ambur station and put on the next train to Madras. All our clothes were torn and I was bleeding from a gash in the forehead above the eyebrow. Lakshman was holding his left arm awkwardly. It had been dislocated at the shoulder. All of us had cuts and bruises and contusions all over and Prof Michael had lost his spectacles and wristwatch. Oh, it was terrible.

Shailaja buried her face in her hands and started sobbing. But she recovered quickly. 'I hope you get those police bastards,' she said fiercely, as she shook hands and walked away.

It seemed to me that Lakshman's experiences with this committee had been the turning point, pushing him from mild anger about injustice into extremist fire to burn all injustice. It metamorphosed him from Lakshman into Shiva.

# Chapter 12

*'Violence is the first resort of the incompetent.'*

—Isaac Asimov in 'Foundation'

There was a soft knocking on the door. It was a little after six in the morning. I opened the door. Two men stood on the steps. One I recognised as one of the most famous surgeons in Madras. He was short, scrawny, balding, head hunched forward and neck drawn in between the shoulders. He looked frightened. He was unimpressive but he had a deft touch with the scalpel and an even surer knack of wringing the last paisa from his patients, rich or poor. A sorry specimen of a man, ethically cauterised. He was known to be filthyrich, with monstrously fat bank balances and secret lockers stuffed with five hundred rupee notes, jewellery and fixed deposit receipts. He flaunted his wealth, probably because he could bank on the patronage of the politicians, bureaucrats and policemen whose gallstones he removed and whose girl friends he relieved of the contents of embarrassingly growing wombs. But he was an expert at his job and renowned internationally.

The story went that once, in the mid eighties, a super-comrade from the Kremlin was struck down by a bad case of haemorrhoids when on a visit to India. He had to be treated in secret because the Kremlin could not publicly admit that the Red Czars are as prone to piles as the meanest moujik. Horror of horrors! If this got out, the CIA would leak it and world's great tabloids would have fun for a week. The Indian government called in our surgical wizard and he was flown to Delhi at night in an Indian Air Force plane. He refused payment for treating the Crimson Rear but the grateful Russian sent him a couple of crates of Royal Salute every month for five years. Our friend, of course, hawked the Scotch in the black market.

The other man was young, of middle height, with curly hair and liquid eyes that were dulled by pain and drugs. He was dark but I could make out the agony-induced pallor underneath the skin. He was dressed in an elegant, double breasted three-piece suit of pearly gray, a light blue shirt and a maroon tie with a diamond tie pin and a handkerchief peeped out of his breast pocket, perfectly shaped into the regulation triangle. A stroke of genius, I thought. Who would expect a desperate Naxalite to dress like Bertie Wooster? I stood aside to let them enter and bolted the door.

As I turned Shiva swayed and was about to fall. I rushed forward and eased him on to the bed. The surgeon quickly unzipped his black bag and took out a sterile disposable syringe. I propped Shiva up against the headboard and removed his coat, tie and shirt. His left side was heavily bandaged and there was blood oozing out of a wound. The surgeon quickly injected something into Shiva's arm. Shiva twisted uneasily and muttered and moaned. Soon, the drug took effect and he slipped into a deep sleep.

I offered the surgeon coffee but he refused brusquely. He was scared and wanted to get away quickly. He took out capsules, a couple of small bottles filled with a pale liquid, half a dozen disposable syringes and some bandages, cotton and dressings from his bag and put them on the table.

He took out a folded sheet of paper from his pocket and asked me to read it. I had detailed instructions about Shiva's medication.

'He has been shot,' the surgeon said. 'It is not too serious, a small caliber bullet in the left side. I have removed it and there don't seem to be signs of infection. You have to change the dressing every eight hours and give him the injections and capsules according to the schedule in the paper. Do you understand?'

I nodded. 'What about his diet?'

'Give him liquids till tomorrow afternoon. Fruit juice, coconut water. Tomorrow evening, give him chicken soup. He needs to regain his strength. He will recover quickly. He is a tough specimen. He should be on his feet in a couple of days. Goodbye.'

The man practically ran to the door. As I let him out, I said: 'Walk normally, doctor. We don't want to attract attention, do we?' He grimaced and walked nervously towards a car parked a few doors away. I bolted the door. Shiva was sleeping peacefully. He did not wake up when I slipped off his trousers, shoes and socks and covered him with a light sheet.

I bathed, breakfasted and sat by Shiva's bed till eleven o'clock. There were some oranges in the kitchen. I made some orange juice with lots of sugar in it and put it in a flask. I wrote a note to Shiva, telling him where he was, that I would be back around five in the evening, that there was orange juice in the flask. For a few moments I wondered how I should sign the note. Then I wrote 'Father' at the bottom and propped the note on the side-table which I moved to where he could reach it. He seemed comfortable enough. I locked my room from the outside and left.

* * *

Shiva was awake when I got back home around six in the evening carrying shopping bags full of bread, soup packets, fruit and vegetables. He was leaning against the headboard of the bed. An uncertain smile crept across his face as I entered. I dropped the shopping bags on the dining table and turned and locked and bolted the door.

Then I walked towards him, smiled and said: 'Hello, son.'

He smiled too, this time with relief, warmth, welcome and reciprocation of welcome. 'Hello, father.'

I laid the back of my hand against his forehead and under his chin to check whether he was running a fever. His body was cool to the touch. I pulled a chair near the bed and sat down. I lit a cigarette. There was still awkwardness in the atmosphere which I wanted to dispel quickly.

I stuck out my hand and said: 'Welcome home, Shiva.'

His face lit up when I called him Shiva. He gripped my hand hard, wordless. I grinned at him and he grinned back. I did not let go of his hand and we looked at each other in silence.

'Hungry?'

He nodded.

I picked up a packet of chicken soup and went to the kitchen. I heated the soup and poured it into a deep bowl. I cut up two slices of bread into small pieces and dropped them into the soup. I made myself a cup of coffee, put the soup and the coffee on a tray and carried it back to the room. Shiva had not moved. He ate the soup in silence as I sipped coffee. He finished the bowl quickly and leaned back with a sigh of satisfaction.

'More?'

'No, thank you, father.'

I took the bowl from his hands and placed it on the table, along with my empty coffee cup.

'How do you feel?'

'Much better, thank you. But a bit weak.'

'You have another day and a half to recover your strength. You will be moved out of here early in the morning the day after tomorrow.'

'Yes, I have been told so.' Shiva leaned back and closed his eyes. 'My mother seems to have worked out everything, to the nth semicolon and the ultimate full stop. As she has always done.'

'Yes,' I said. 'She was always very efficient.'

Shiva laughed softly. 'Don't I know!'

'Are you comfortable? Shall I get you another pillow?'

'I'm fine, thank you, father.'

He woke up only the next morning, a little past eight o'clock. I was sitting in a chair next to the bed, gazing at his face when he opened his eyes.

'Good morning,' I said.

He sat up, with a slight grimace of pain.

'Don't you think you should rest some more?'

'No father, I'm much better now. The pain has gone, almost.'

Shiva swung his legs off the bed and stood up. A flicker of pain crossed his face but he seemed to have recovered very quickly from his injuries. He felt his side, pressed it over the bandages and grimaced again. He walked towards the bathroom with a firm stride. He was young and strong and full of purpose.

I made coffee for both of us and we drank it in silence as he read the newspapers and I watched him fondly and with pride.

'You see', he said, his face now serious, 'Lies, nothing but lies. Our whole society is founded on a base of untruth and propped up by lies. The whole structure has to be brought down and rebuilt.'

'You may be right, chum. But you are going to have a bloody tough time doing it. In my view, it is impossible; at least in the near future. You and your revolutionaries are too small in number, too weak, too disunited, and too scattered. You can be packed off individually in police actions and none will shed a tear, even as many applaud. You see, they are all hypocrites. The police and the state raise the bogey of violence and the common man will roar for your destruction. But let a pig stray into a mosque or a cow's tail be tweaked in front of a temple and the same apostles of non-violence who sanction your killing, will kick and maul and batter and stab their neighbours in mad blood lust. I'm sure you see my point. It's not the violence of you and your comrades to which they really object. It is the fact that their passions are not aroused by the injustice that you are fighting against. Religion is a far more powerful motivator than injustice, which anyway is happening to the other man and not to me.'

I continued, 'And then there is the fact that Marx got it absolutely right. 'Workers of the world unite, you have nothing to lose but your chains.' It is precisely when people have nothing, absolutely nothing but their chains to lose, that they will rise in revolution. Read Mao, read Ho Chi Minh, read Castro, read the history of China and Vietnam. Revolution occurs only when there is chaos all around. When there is even the slightest semblance of order, man prefers to stay at home and eat and get drunk and make love to his wife. He will take up his knife and his gun only when there is absolutely no other way out. And that time has not come. Nor will it ever come in India, I think.'

Shiva had been listening patiently, intently. He must have heard the same things many, many times before but showed not the slightest sign of impatience or irritability.

'Oh, I agree with much of what you say', he said, 'especially the hypocrisy about violence. I must tell you about this orgy of violence which happened right before my eyes.'

'There were two farmers in Korattur village, one a rich landlord called Kandaswamy Naicker, and the other a marginal farmer, Karuppiah. Naicker had gone over to Karuppiah's fields to look at a bull which Karuppiah was selling to raise money for his daughter's wedding. Naicker was inspecting the bull when it tossed its horns. Naicker was too close; he was in fact quite drunk and could not move out of the way fast enough. The horn ripped out Naicker's left eye. The man ran howling back to his house. Within minutes, Naicker's two sons came running with their sickles. The elder son cut off the bull's head while the younger ripped Karuppiah's belly open. I rushed and grappled with the younger son. This man was insane with rage. As we fought he tried to kill me too. Finally I was able to kick him in the crotch and he collapsed. In the meantime, the elder son had slit Karuppiah's throat and came at me. By that time, several villagers came running and stopped him. I insisted that the two sons should be tied up and handed over to the police. The villagers were afraid of reprisals. One by one they slunk away. The two sons stood there laughing at me. And then they came at me again. I was alone and unarmed. I knew that they were out to kill me. I turned and ran.'

'What happened, then?' I asked. 'Didn't the police arrest the two sons for the murder of Karuppiah?'

'Oh father, you are so naïve. Your cloak of cynicism is threadbare. How do you expect the police to arrest the two sons of the richest landlord? That day may come, it has to come, maybe when my grandchildren are old.'

Shiva stood up and walked around a bit, lifting his arms chest high and swinging them slowly from side to side, testing his ribs. He did not seem to be in much pain.

He sat down on the bed. 'And then, there are the socio-economic arguments why revolution is inevitable in this country. The poor are getting progressively poorer and as the population explodes the ranks of the semi-starving are going to swell further, in terms of absolutes numbers. I don't have to explain all this to you in detail. But one factor may have escaped your notice. The globalisation of the Indian economy, which started in 1991, is slowly but surely, helping our cause. The government is encouraging investment for the elite and the middle class consumption ignoring, generally, the agricultural sector. The same old land relations and production relations that accentuate poverty, turn marginal farmers into landless labourers and push landless labourers deeper into debt with moneylenders. The one vital fact of modern history that the government, whichever party is in power, has missed is that the more you improve the economic lot of the poor; the less is the chance of revolution. That's where your insight about having absolutely nothing to lose but chains, is so important. Why has there been no revolution in Britain or the USA, though in the nineteenth century the conditions of the workers there were as bad as those of our peasants today? Because the ruling elite were sensible enough to ensure first that the poor got food, clothing and shelter and later education, television sets, fast cars and Coca-cola. A full stomach smothers revolution.'

'You know, Shiva, one curious thing strikes me and I love you the more for it. You don't talk like any of the communists I have met. You have been talking for the past twenty minutes and not once have you used words like bourgeois, revisionist, comprador or left opportunism.'

Shiva laughed. 'Oh, I can spout stuff like that for hours on end, and in Tamil too. I read and annotated the complete works of Marx, Engels, Lenin and Mao in one year. And I've got a memory like a camera. Mother thought I would chant Keynes and Friedman like Bertie Wooster reciting 'The Wreck of Hesperus' or Viswanatha Sastrigal, the Rig Veda. Poor mother.'

'Poor mother, indeed. Poor me, rather.'

He laughed again. 'Okay, Pops, forget the past. I knew I would impress you only if I used ordinary English and not jargon.'

'Thanks for small mercies, Shiva. Jargon would indeed have given me migraine. Now, it's time for your medicines. And take rest. Eat. Sleep. Recover your strength fully. You can't afford to waste your energy now.'

'You're right, father.'

'I'll heat up some soup for you. After that you lie down. You're not getting up till it's time to leave.'

Shiva rested the whole day. I went to the office, locking him in. I returned home a little after seven. We dined on rice, rasam, papad and curds. We were asleep by ten o'clock.

We were up by five in the morning. Shiva bathed and dressed in the Bertie Wooster outfit. We waited, I chain-smoking and he as still as a stone idol. Renuka's goons came an hour later. I hugged him and he left.

# Chapter 13

*'Some silly idiot walked across the screen just as the ball was bowled.'*

—Mike in 'Psmith in the City' by P G Wodehouse

'Two questions, Bharat,' said Dr Hekyll.

'Yes, two questions,' echoed Mr Jyde.

'And what are they?'

'Oh, both are pretty obvious,' said Mr Jyde. 'They should be obvious to even our friend in the Treasury benches and I will allow him to ask the first one.'

Dr Hekyll was jumping up and down on the optic nerve behind my right eye. 'Mr Speaker, Sir, you cannot allow such insulting behaviour to continue.'

'Okay, I'll do it,' said Mr Jyde. 'The first question is: Did you ask Shiva who shot him?'

I replied: 'Yes, I did. That was an obvious question to ask, wasn't it?'

Dr Hekyll: 'And who did shoot him?'

'His mother, of course,' I said. 'There was no other way for her to immobilise him long enough for her hoodlums to whisk him away. And the second question?'

Mr Jyde: 'When are you going to answer the question you asked in the first chapter of this book? About wearing the bottoms of your trousers rolled?

'Wait, Mr Jyde,' said Dr Hekyll. 'It will come in the fullness of time. Rome wasn't built in a day, you know?'

# Chapter 14

*'I have smelt them, the death bringers...I have smelt corruption in the dish, incense in the latrine, the sewer in the incense....'*

—'Murder in the Cathedral'—T S Eliot

I was arrested a few days after Shiva left. I was taken to a two-storeyed house with a huge garden in the northern suburbs of the city. Ignatius Nathan, deputy inspector general of police, in charge of anti-terrorist activities, was standing on the steps of the house. 'Welcome, Dr Bharat Sharma,' he said. 'I am going to torture you.'

I was dragged into a room in which there was a large table with two chairs on opposite sides. Nathan pushed me into one of them, went round the table and sat in the other one.

'Torture,' said Nathan,' is the infliction of severe physical pain and/or mental stress on a prisoner against his will. That is the definition of torture given to me at a course in interrogation techniques that I attended a couple of years ago in Belfast. The instructors were British army experts. I am going to inflict severe mental stress on you, obviously against your will. Therefore, over the next 48 hours—I don't think you'll last longer, you're much too soft—I am going to torture you.'

The man was tremendously sure of himself. Why was he telling me all this, letting me know what was coming, allowing me to prepare myself? Or had the process of torture already begun? Yes, that must be it. He had already started. He had begun the process of putting me under extreme mental stress by building on my fears. It was subtle; God! It was subtle. He had somehow sensed that though I was an intellectual and had never really experienced physical agony, the classical methods of inflicting pain would not work with me. He wanted information quickly about the whereabouts of my son, but the parental bond is too strong to be snapped in a few days through a broken body. Moreover, he did not want to mark me; no smashed ribs, missing teeth, twisted limbs that would force the world to believe me if I later claimed that I had been tortured. He wanted me to talk now and remain silent or, at least, sound incredible later. So it was my mind that had to be broken. My life was lived in the mind; my existence is defined by logic, language and the process of ratiocination. He began with a definition, since logic is a process of building up constructs, one on top of another, starting with a premise which has to be accurately defined. He was getting into my mind on the ground floor, empathising so that my consciousness would vibrate to the rhythm set by him, controlled by him and capable of being shattered by him. I had to work out my response, my defence. It was certain he was going the mental route. But I could not afford to shut out the possibility of a surprise riposte at the flesh, a sudden shift to excruciating pain as a counterpoint, in the face of the suddenness and agony of which I might collapse. I had to be prepared, but at the lower levels of consciousness, so that the deep recesses of the brain could resist without prompting when the attack came. My defence would be with the tools of the mind, my brain, my sense of humour and the sarcasm and cynicism instilled through the 5,000 years of existence of the Thanjavur Paapaan.

'Torture is such a crude word', I said, smiling. 'Surely, you would prefer a more dignified and detached term. Scientific interrogation, for instance?'

'Torture is good enough for you and for me, my friend', Nathan said with a grin as he switched on the powerful lamp on the table and centered it, so that the light blazed directly into my face. I was blinded and brought my forearm up to protect my eyes. The blindness lasted a few moments as my eyes adjusted themselves to the photon level and then I could make out the dim hulk of the policeman standing on the other side of the table. The heat began to pierce through and sweat gushed out of my pores, pouring in rivulets down my forehead through my eyebrows and into my eyes. I brushed the sweat away with the back of my hand. Nathan came quickly round the desk, forced my arms behind the chair and handcuffed them. Now I could not wipe away the sweat that sluiced into my eyes. The salt stung and I blinked furiously.

'Allow me to expatiate a little on the theory and practice of torture,' Nathan said as he moved back to this chair.

'I have already defined the term.' His voice took on the tone I had used in my lectures several lifetimes ago. 'I will not describe too thoroughly the methods to be used. You're going to experience them anyway in, let me see, in exactly half an hour from now. It is 3.28 p.m. We shall begin at 3.58 p.m. on the dot.'

Nathan slipped off his wristwatch and placed it at the centre of the table, propping it up at an angle with a paperweight so that the dial was visible to me, even through the glare of the lamp.

I needed to hit back. I ripped off a variation of a limerick I had learnt as an undergraduate.

*'Ignatius Nathan, a policeman brave,*

*Kept a dead whore in a cave.*

*He said I admit*

*I'm a bit of a shit;*

*But think of the money I save.'*

He laughed. 'That's a good one. I haven't heard it before. Keep it up. I'm going to enjoy the next two days. Now, where was I? Yes, the theory and practice of torture. First, we have to describe how torture works and why it is so effective. I am not a teacher like you were and my own words are too feeble a medium. So I'll read to you from one of the better books on the subject. You might want to make a mental note of the title. It will be useful reference material for the series of articles on India as a police State, which I am sure you will want to write when you are released. The book is called 'The technology of political control' and it was written by four British activists.'

He placed a sheet of paper on the table and started reading from it. 'Initial responses to stress are fairly well understood. When someone encounters a dangerous or frightening situation, the characteristic response of the body is to prepare itself for aggressive action or flight. The adrenal glands produce more adrenaline and the muscles and the brain work at peak efficiency.'

Nathan came round the table once again and, putting his mouth close to my ear, whispered: 'Don't you feel your heart beating more strongly and your head strangely clear? Don't you feel utterly confident now that you can withstand anything that I can do to you? Don't you feel strong enough to climb Mount Everest? Aren't your hands and your legs and your stomach and your chest and your cock pulsating with powerful impulses? Don't fool yourself, my friend. It is not the strength of the mind or the eternal will or the boundless determination of the human soul to fight injustice and resist murderous assaults on human dignity and freedom. It's just a chemical reaction. Your adrenal gland is pumping quantities of adrenaline into your body. It will not last long. See what the specialists on the subject have to say.'

He went back to his chair and started reading again from the sheet of paper. 'If the stressful situation lasts for a longer period of time, this typical acute response cannot be maintained. Provided individuals see themselves as acting purposefully in the situation, they can maintain effectiveness (in military terms, morale) for a considerable period of time. But at a cost: they suffer anxiety, sleeplessness and loss of appetite. Eventually, breakdown into a chronic state occurs.'

Nathan put away the paper and took another. 'Now let me read to you a description of a man who was tortured by the KGB. Here goes: He sits and stares with a vacant expression, perhaps endlessly twisting a button on his coat. He allows himself to become dirty and disheveled. He no longer bothers about the niceties of eating. He mixes the food into a mush and stuffs it into his mouth like an animal. He goes through the prison routine automatically, as if he were in a daze. The slop jar is no longer offensive to him. Ultimately he may lose some of the restraints of ordinary behaviour. He may soil himself. He weeps, he mutters, he prays aloud.'

Once again Nathan moved around to my chair and placed his hands on my shoulders from behind. His voice was conversational, friendly. 'You know, Dr Bharat Sharma, the aftereffects of torture are not, I repeat not, temporary. They could be—in most cases, they are—permanent. You see, torture creates in the victim an abnormal state of mind in which the experience of torture, the trauma as the shrinks call it, takes a near-total hold of the mind of the victim. A famous psychologist described the symptoms thus: spells of uncontrollable emotions, especially of anxiety and frequently of rage, occasionally even convulsive attacks, sleeplessness or dreams in which the trauma is experienced again and again, also mental repetitions during the day of the traumatic situations and diminished sexual interest. Surely you don't want to end up as a nut case? Surely you don't want to be impotent with the delectable Jennifer Jones? Why don't you just tell us what we want to know and go away, a sane, peaceful man?'

His hands still rested slightly on my shoulders.

'Mr Nathan,' I said, 'I do not know anything about where Shiva is, what he is doing, what has been done to him. I know nothing. All your efforts, and I must compliment you on your technique, will be wasted. At the end of it all, my answer will be the same: I know nothing. And, by the way, I heard you recently bought a Maruti car. Then, this joke should make you laugh. Why are Maruti cars like haemorrhoids? You don't know? Because, sometime or the other, every arsehole gets them. Good, don't you think?

Nathan's hands slipped around my throat. He leaned over and squeezed. 'I'm going to break you, you bastard. It will give me the greatest pleasure. When I'm done with you, you'll be all broken inside. I'll leave you a vegetable.' He squeezed harder, till my head pounded intolerably and my vision dimmed. He let go and I fell forwards. I was almost unconscious. He unlocked the handcuffs and hauled me up. 'Time for your treatment,' he said and hauled me out of the room.

# Chapter 15

*'There is a crime here that goes beyond denunciation. There is a sorrow here that weeping cannot symbolise....the grapes of wrath are filling and growing heavy, growing heavy for the vintage.'*

—'The Grapes of Wrath', John Steinbeck

I was taken down to a room in the basement. It had an electronically operated door which opened when Nathan touched a button in the wall. As we went in, the door closed automatically. There was a thick pile-carpet and the walls and ceiling were covered with some plastic material which looked curiously bloated.

There was a cot bolted to the floor in the middle of the room. There was a mattress on the cot but no pillow. Straps were attached to the frame, six of them at intervals of a foot along the length of the cot.

Nathan was looking closely at my face, gauging my reactions. 'This is a totally sound-proofed room. You won't hear anything even if I set off a grenade outside the door.'

'Nor can anyone outside hear the screams of the victim, I suppose?' My face twisted with disgust.

'We're not bothered about that. No one who is not authorised can get within hearing distance of this room. And those who are authorised would not be bothered. This is part of the 'treatment'. Your being here has a two-fold purpose. One is to get information about your son and the other is to continue testing certain techniques of interrogation we have picked up from our more civilised cousins in the West. What I am going to try on you is a much speeded up version of solitary confinement. It is called sensory deprivation.'

For the first time in the afternoon, I was afraid. I remembered reading something about this modern method of torture. I knew that it destroyed the victims' minds in most cases, leaving them psychotic wrecks, out of synchronisation with reality. It would take years of the best psychiatric care to bring them back to normal and even then the odds were long. For a moment, I wondered whether it was worth risking my sanity to protect a man whom I had known closely only for a few days. But he was my son and he deserved every chance he could get. Anyway, I was not going to hold out for too long. Only two days. By then he would either be free or joining me in the same room. Would two days be too long for my mind? How would I know when the two days were over?

Nathan piled on the pressure.

'A pretty little thing, this sensory deprivation technique. It is based on the need of the human brain to be active all the time. Even in sleep, the brain and the mind are at work.

That is why you dream. To be active, the brain needs new sensory and perceptual inputs all the time; the common sights and sounds of daily life, the susurrations of a fan, the hum of an air-conditioner, the hard or soft feel of a chair or a bed, the sight of a coffee cup on the breakfast table or light glinting off a window pane, the smell of food or a woman's perfume or a man's sweat. In sensory deprivation torture, the victim is cut off from all sounds, sights, smells and tastes. The sense of touch is reduced to the minimum.'

Nathan opened a closet with a sliding door set flush in one wall and took out a strait-jacket. He ordered me to strip completely and get into the strait-jacket. When I was done, he made me cross my arms in front and looped the long sleeves behind my back and tied-strapped them so that I could barely move my hands and arms.

He made me sit on the bed and took out what looked like black cloth bag from the closet. This is the hood. It has been used with incredible effect on IRA prisoners in Belfast. As you can see, it is made of tightly woven black cloth which cuts off all light, so that the brain gets no impulses through the eyes. The room will, of course, be totally darkened when I leave. You will be strapped down on the bed: the mattress is made of special material so that your sense of touch is reduced to the minimum possible. You'll feel as if you are floating in mid air. You will not be able to move. You will not hear anything because the room is sound-proofed. No taste either, since you will get no food or water. This is the most effective method of scientific interrogation since it leaves no physical marks. All this, of course, is to soften you up for questions. And don't think you will escape by sleeping; your brain will not allow you to sleep.'

'You see, all new perceptual input will be cut off. But the brain continues working. Lacking new sensations, it will substitute internally generated information, which is what the madman does. The subjects of such torture then suffer all kinds of subjective experiences. Thinking becomes disordered; you hallucinate. You will not know where exactly your arms and legs are. You may think that your head is a cone spinning away from your body like a satellite released from a spacecraft. You will get nightmares and you will be filled with paranoid fears: the floor is swarming with poisonous snakes and a deadly scorpion is crawling along your nose to peck out your eyes. All these produce what is technically defined as anxiety which brings on more bizarre experiences. You panic but there is no release. When there is no release and not even the prospect of release, you find yourself utterly helpless. Under such conditions, a full-blown acute psychotic condition can be induced in three or four days.'

I had been looking steadily at his face as he talked. 'Making me a psychotic is not going to help you. How can you be sure that what I will tell you is the truth and not a fabrication of my sickened imagination or the vaporous froth of a ruined mind?'

'We have our ways. And anyway, getting information out of you is of secondary importance. My main purpose is to continue testing the effectiveness of the sensory deprivation technique in our country, how good it is for use on the Indian psyche, how long it takes to break one of our people using this method. So I wouldn't be heart-broken if, at the end of it, what you tell me about Shiva is of little use.'

'You animal,' I screamed, my self control breaking for the first time. 'If I get out sane, I will hunt you down and kill. You can't escape me, run where you will. I'll cut your balls off and watch you die slowly. I'll...I'll...' I stopped with an effort. There was no point in shouting.

Nathan had been watching me with a pleased smile. 'Right, professor yellow journalist, time to get cracking.' He slipped the hood over my head. It came down to my shoulders and was tight-fitting, made of some fabric that molded itself to my flesh and bones. For a minute or two I could feel the cloth, but soon there was little sensation. I thought I could faintly make out the light from the overhead bulb. But it was only my imagination, the hope of the brain that I could, after all, get some visual inputs, even if it was only for a few minutes till Nathan put out the lights and left the room. He strapped me down to the bed so that I could not make the slightest movement. The straps were made of some soft material which I could not feel through the strait-jacket and they were tied tightly enough to totally restrict movement. I found that I could move the muscles in my arms and legs by constricting and releasing them. It might be useful to do that occasionally; that much of new sensation would enter my brain. I could hear faint noises as Nathan's feet brushed the carpet as he left the room. Then, all was silence.

At first, it was a deafening silence. There was an alternating roar and hum in my ears but I knew that my brain had started hunting for new impulses. Bright colored flashes of light lashed at my eyes; it happens when you press your fingers on your closed eyelids. I let myself relax totally; regulating my breathing in the style of the yoga exercises I had learnt long ago. I had forgotten the prescribed rhythm and I made up one. Count eight while inhaling and fourteen while exhaling; suck in your stomach as the breath eases out of your lungs.

Soon I was totally relaxed physically. I felt as if I were floating on air or on the surface of a gentle swell in the sea. I remembered my long bathes in the Bay of Bengal, off Elliot's Beach, when I used to float on my back for hours. I thought I could hear the gentle roar of the waves and the sound of children playing excitedly at the water's edge. I don't know how long this went on, how long I was warmly enveloped in nothingness. It was luxuriously, deliciously pleasant and I wondered whether Nathan and all the other Torquemadas of the twentieth century were totally wrong. Or was I the unique soul which could withstand, and even revel in, this supposedly devilish form of torture? But the thought soon vanished into the vacuum of outer space in which I was an ethereal gossamer. 'We are such stuff as dreams are made of.'

After a while, I was a fish in the ocean, sinking slowly down to dark depths, to the bottom of the Challenger Deep, where I crossed my fins in the lotus position and meditated upon the Infinite as I chanted the words 'Coca Cola' again and again. I was the Matsyavatara, waiting for the deluge at the end of the Yuga, waiting to open my mouth and drink up the oceans.

I snapped out of it with a mental start. This is it, I thought. It has begun. Time to fight. I had read that a victim of solitary confinement had once catalogued 27,000 words in his head to retain hold of the frail thread of sanity. I decided I would recite aloud the famous speeches of Shakespeare. I went through To be or not to be; Friends, Romans and countrymen; Canst thou not minister to the mind diseased; Is this a dagger that I see before me; Antony's speech to the troops at Philippi; bits and pieces of Othello, The Tempest, Coriolanus. Then I went through The Rape of the Lock, Here thou, great Anna whom three realms obey, doth sometimes counsel take and sometimes tea. But soon I realised that it was a mistake to recite aloud; I felt thirsty and my throat became parched. I swallowed what saliva I could summon up and went on reciting mentally. I switched to limericks, which have always delighted me; I have a whole library in my head. I started with the limerick that defines the limerick.

*A limerick packs laughs anatomical*
*In space that is quite economical;*
*But the good ones I've seen*
*So seldom are clean*
*And the clean ones so seldom are comical.*

I chuckled and probed my memory for the clean and comical ones.

*A fly and a flea in a flue*
*Were imprisoned, so what could they do?*
*Said the fly, let us flee;*
*Said the flea, let us fly.*
*And together they flew out of the flue.*

Soon I ran out of the clean ones.

*There was a man from Nigeria,*
*Whose morals were a bit inferior;*
*He did to a nun,*
*What shouldn't be done,*
*Now she's a mother superior.*

*There was a young lady of Starkey,*
*Who had an affair with a darkie;*
*The results of her sins,*
*Were quadruplets, not twins,*
*One white, one black and two khaki.*

I smiled as I remembered the reaction of a first year English class to which I let off this one without warning at the start of the first lecture. The students ate out of my hands for the rest of the year, though I got a dressing down from the head of the English department. I remembered two which I had read in an American novel, two 'literary' limericks.

*A bawd in a brothel did waken*

*To find all her sex organs achin.'*

*She thought all that rough screwing*

*Was bald, bearded Will's doing*

*But really it was Sir Francis Bacon.*

And the other one.

*Blind Milton leaving God in the skies,*

*Leapt on his wife by surprise.*

*He said 'Dear, I can't see*

*It but if you'll just pee*

*It will help me find Paradise.'*

A mental laugh that reverberated in the cerebral cortex and a stream of consciousness slid into Housman. Malt did more than Milton ever could to justify the ways of God to Man. Our Father, that art in Heaven, hallowed be thy Name, thy Kingdom come, thy kingdom will come when Kalki comes riding a white horse to Banbury Cross, with bells on his fingers and rings on his toes, he'll be riding down the mountain, when he comes he'll come in this Kali Yuga too, he promised didn't he, to establish Dharma? Paritranaya Sadhunam Vinasayacha Dushkritam Dharma Samsthapanaya Sambhavami Yuge Yuge, I was Arjuna twanging the bowstring of the Gandiva in triumph and challenging the primordial Om vibrating to the divine ululation of Krishna's conch sitting at Krishna's feet as he recited the Bhagavad Gita, which he had learnt from Veda Vyasa. Krishna's face was black, as it should be, but why was he mustachioed, why was it Nathan rocketing my chariot towards Jayadratha whom I had sworn to destroy before sunset or kill myself if I failed? Oh God, the sun has set and Nathan is still alive. The sun has set and I'm hungry Jenny, bring on the pepper steak and the red wine.

My stomach growled with hunger. From this I deduced that six to eight hours must have passed since Nathan left the room. The hunger became a constant ache in the stomach. Waves of nausea rose to my throat as the fragrance of frying potato curry wafted across my nostrils and sharp bouquet of milagu rasam scurried into my nose and through to the back of my tongue, activating the taste buds. Saliva spurted into my mouth. I swallowed and a vision of a rivulet tricking into nothingness in a burning desert filled my eyes. Full many a flower is born to blush unseen and waste its sweetness on the desert air.

My stomach twisted with a cramp of hunger and I clamped down with the mind, shutting off the agony, yoga-breathing again and I drifted off. Yet once more into the breach dear friends. My bladder filled up and I desperately wanted to urinate. I tried to get up and go to the bathroom. Why couldn't I get up? What's happening? Look I want to piss badly let me go or I'll do it in bed and mother will be very angry.

Hold on. Hang on. This is good. The urge to urinate is a real sensation, a fresh input for your brain to work on, to keep you sane. But my brain wants to piss too. Mother and Father told my brain that it should piss regularly you shouldn't hold back you'll wet your shorts and people will laugh at you. You are grown up now, you're five years old. My son's a big boy now and he'll piss only in the toilet won't he? There's a good boy.

Warm fluid flowing into my crotch, soaking my shorts, blessed release, delicious rising stench of uric acid, sensual, sexual.

I do not remember much more about how I went through those two days. The defensive mechanism of the mind went into action, I suppose, blanking out the horror. But there is one bizarre hallucination that keeps breaking through the protective shroud of a deliberately defective memory, which brings back the terror and horror in regular nightmares even now. My body had turned into separate masses of vegetables, rotting, decaying in a garbage can in my bedroom, the head a pumpkin, the trunk a Brobdingnagian capsicum, the legs and arms giant cucumbers, my testicles little tomatoes. My soul said 'I can't bear it, this perfume gives me a headache' and darted out of my ears which were slices of beetroot in a salad bowl and scurried towards the ceiling where it sat and crossed its legs and stared at me. It croaked like a crow and metamorphosed into an owl which peered at me with wise curiosity, hooting all the while. Then it became a vulture which wanted to peck my eyes out. The vulture had Nathan's face and Renuka's breasts as it swooped down, claws curved to tear the hood away and attack my eyes. I screamed as I felt a hand on my neck and the hood was gone and a blinding light pierced my eyes and cauterised my brain and I passed out.

# Chapter 16

*Those worlds, covered with blind darkness, are 'Sunless' by name.*

—Isa Uanishad, Verse 3

I was lying on the cot in the torture chamber when I regained consciousness. My face, neck and shoulders were sopping wet; someone had thrown a bucket of water on me. I licked the drops that flowed past my lips and tried to open my eyes. The light was still too bright and I closed my eyes again. Someone put his arms under my armpits and hauled me up, first into a sitting position and then made me stand. He let go his hands and I collapsed in a heap on the floor. I was pulled up again, this time by two pairs of hands and taken out of the room, my feet dragging uselessly on the floor. They half-carried, half-pulled me up the stairs to the room in which Nathan had lectured me on the theory and practice of torture. I was dumped into a chair. My head lolled against the backrest while my legs twisted themselves around the legs of the chair to keep me from falling forward. I opened my eyes again and now I could see without too much pain.

Nathan was sitting across the table, peering at me clinically, taking in first impressions of the effects of his technique. A tape recorder was running on the table. There was an open packet of cigarettes and a box of matches on the table. With a great languor slowing me down so that I felt I was swimming underwater, I straightened, took out a cigarette, put it between my lips, picked up the match box, extracted a match and tried to light it. My hands started shaking uncontrollably and I could not get the match-head to strike the box and ignite. Nathan leaned across, took the box from my hand and lit the cigarette. I sucked in the smoke gratefully, drew it deep into my lungs and let it out, the smoke trickling in wisps out of my nostrils. A couple of more puffs and I felt infinitely better. There was a glass of water on the table and I took a few sips.

'Did you have a good time, Dr Sharma,' asked Nathan.

'Passable, Mr Nathan, passable.' My voice was a hoarse croak.

'Are you ready to talk now?'

'What day is it? What is the time?'

'Why do you want to know?'

'Okay, back to the dungeon it is.'

'It is a little past 4 p.m. on Thursday. You have been in the hood for forty-eight hours.'

'Get anything interesting?'

'Oh yes,' said Nathan enthusiastically. 'A treasure house of research material. We were monitoring you throughout. Visually, using infra red light and electronically for audio and physiological data. The hood and the straitjacket have minute electrodes which you cannot feel.'

I yawned. 'As one guinea pig said to another, it's all in a good cause. Or, to think of it, like the actress said to the bishop.' I felt light-headed, gay, slightly drunk, more because of the headiness of success than the torture session; or so I told myself.

Nathan was getting impatient. 'I repeat my question. Are you ready to talk?'

'Am I ready to talk? I suppose so. By now, my son will either be free and out of the country or you would have arrested him. Either way, it doesn't matter if I talk freely now.'

'Right,' said Nathan, rubbing his hands. 'Do you want me to ask questions or will you make a statement?'

'I'll make a statement. That will be quicker.'

Nathan checked whether the tape recorder was running and said: 'You may begin.'

I gave him a quick account of what had happened since Renuka told me Shiva had become a Naxalite. It took about fifteen minutes. Nathan played the tape back to me in case I wanted to make any corrections. I did not. He said he would get the tape transcribed so that I could sign a typed statement. He went out of the room and I leaned back in the chair and stretched my legs. I slept.

Nathan shook me awake. I read through the typescript of my statement and signed four copies. Nathan gave me one. I tore it up and let the pieces fall on the floor.

'What happens now?' I asked. 'Are you going to arrest me and produce me before a magistrate?'

Nathan shook his head. 'No. It is not worth the trouble. You are a journalist and your friends in the gutter Press can create a lot of trouble for us. You are free to go.'

I stood up, pressing my hands on the arms of the chair to give me the impetus to rise. I was not sure I could walk without support. But I found that I could, if I walked slowly. Strength was returning to my legs. I refused Nathan's offer to drop me home in a police car and walked out of that abode of evil.

I walked along the road, looking for a taxi or an auto rickshaw.

I was in a blind rage and yet, a part of me was philosophical. I felt I was two persons inhabiting one mind; the first swore vengeance, the second tried to analyse and understand what had been done to me.

I wanted to go back and tear Nathan's heart out with my bare hands.

I told myself that what they had done to me was what Man had been doing to Man since the time we climbed down from the trees and walked on two legs instead of four.

I was outraged that they did not feel the least bit guilty about their excruciating intrusion into my innermost self.

A part of me said: 'Shut up, what else did you expect? By their lights, what they did was justifiable.'

I, Bharat Sharma, draw upon the power of five thousand years of culture, civilisation and intelligence to curse the bastards, may they die of gangrene of the penis.

For them, the justification was in the age-old argument which permits one human being to inflict intolerable pain and even the ultimate accident, death, on another human being: they were only doing their jobs, they were only following orders. Their job was to protect human society in its present form, guarding it from the depredations of those who would change it to a form abhorrent to the current elite. Status Quo was the name of their God and their Prophet and their Head Priest. Maintaining Status Quo was the ritual by which they propitiated their Trinity and the ritual demanded human sacrifice.

I, Bharat Sharma, draw upon the power of five thousand years of culture, civilisation and intelligence to curse the whoresons, may they die of cancer of the testicles.

The ritual was most rigidly practiced when those demanding change, like Shiva and his friends, found force to be the only effective weapon in their armory. When the minority uses force, it is violence; when the majority uses force, it is maintaining law and order. It is a simple equation, taught in secondary school classrooms. Who am I to question this received wisdom?

I, Bharat Sharma, draw upon the power of five thousand years of culture, civilisation and intelligence to curse the motherfuckers, may they die slowly and in terrible pain, fouling their beds with none to help them.

Shiva was a criminal not because a judge in a black gown had pronounced him to be so but because Nathan and his policemen and their employers—you, me and the man in the street—had decreed him to be so. Shiva had been tried and convicted, not by a court, but by the police and the State and those who controlled the State. His 'conviction' would be hailed by all. The only rite that remained to be performed was enforcing the prescribed punishment, prescribed not in the statutes or judges' pronouncements but by that ancient law which said that any member of the tribe who fouled the communal cave must be cast out in to the wilderness beyond death.

I, Bharat Sharma, atheist from the age of 14, now believe in God. For, I believe Nathan and his tribe will burn in Hell or Narakam in everlasting fire.

They were so sure of themselves that they did not even utter the usual warnings about not writing about what had been done to me. They knew, and I knew, that there was no proof. They had not damaged me physically. Only my mind had been assaulted and the damage was invisible. They were safe. Even if I did convince my editor to print what I wrote, they would slap a massive libel case against us and the *Herald*. I could even be labelled a psychotic with a persecution complex and be locked away in a madhouse. No, they knew and I knew that I would never write about the last two days. Anyway, no one would believe it; we do not want to acknowledge the evil that is being done in our name.

Even I could not fully believe that it had happened. The defence mechanism of my mind had already started working and I began to wonder if it had all been a bad dream. I felt weak, the muscles in my thighs and calves quivered continuously but I was able to walk.

A few hundred yards away I stopped a cruising autorickshaw and got in. The driver asked me where I wanted to go. I found that I did not remember the address of my house. I felt a surge of panic and hatred contorted my face. Those bastards have destroyed my mind, I screamed soundlessly.

'Are you all right, mister? Are you ill? Do you want a doctor?' The autorickshaw driver sounded scared and solicitous.

I shook my head. Then I remembered. '29, North Mada Street, Mylapore.' I leaned back and closed my eyes. I must have slept during the hour-long drive from near Ennore to Mylapore, for the driver had to shake me awake when we reached home. I gave him two hundred rupee notes and went in without waiting for the change.

I made myself a cup of black coffee, poured in a slug of rum and hobbled to a chair. I was able to get in only a couple of sips of the scalding drink before a great nausea rose within me. I staggered to the bathroom and vomited violently into the wash basin. It seemed as if my insides were being wrenched out, forced up through my oesophagus and throat and spewed out. But only a thin liquid, blackish green, gushed out. All the evil of the past two days seemed to be boiling forth and out of me. I washed my mouth and face and turned. But I could not walk. My legs seemed to be tubular, hollow. I folded with a groan and fainted on the bathroom floor.

I was unconscious for more than two hours. Then, from a great distance away, thunder pounded. I thought it came from deep within my head, from the recesses of my brain where synapses met and clashed and sparked in a devilish rhythm. It is the dance of death, I thought, and I welcomed it. Then the thunder approached me from deep inside, rushing at my eyes and I cringed in fear and horror. It rushed onwards, exploding through my skull, my eyes, my ears, my nostrils and roared away into the outer void where on the Black Holes live. But even then it stayed near and pounded away at me. Then the terrible ball of sound shattered and resolved itself into separate pieces that I could make out as the noises of someone hammering at the front door and shouting my name. I sat up and, holding on to the wash basin, dragged myself upright. My head seemed clear. The tumor had burst and the pus drained away.

'Coming,' I shouted, but it came out as a hoarse rasp. I staggered to the front door and opened it. Renuka stood there.

'Come in,' I said and shambled to a chair.

'Are you all right?' asked Renuka. 'You look terrible. Where have you been for the last two days? Cataleptic drunk, I suppose. I was getting frantic.' It came out in a rush, a society housewife whining at her servant.

'Pour me a drink.'

Renuka stared at me in shock but moved quietly to the table as she sensed a deadly undertone in my voice. She poured some rum into a glass, added water from the mud pot and handed me the drink.

I downed half the glass in one glug-glugging swallow. There was a minor heave of protest in my stomach but the liquor stayed down. I finished the rest of the glass and felt infinitely better.

'Oh, it was nothing; just the tender, loving ministrations of the police. I was 'interrogated' for two days about Shiva. Those chaps are bloody good at their job. Some pretty refinements that Nathan picked up in London and Belfast, watching his white cousins at work.'

Renu looked worried but her concern was not for me. 'I hope you didn't tell them anything vital?'

'Don't you know me? Smiley and Sean Connery and Roger Moore and Simon Templar, the four-in-one hero.'

'Don't joke with me. Tell me what happened,' Renuka ordered.

'Don't you raise your voice, you bitch,' I shouted. Renuka rocked back, shocked at the venom that lashed at her.

'I don't want to talk about it. Once was bad enough. I'm not going to relive a descent into hell for your pleasure, Renuka. In the end, I talked. It was the only way to get out of there sane, or even alive. I told them all I knew.'

I raised my hand to silence her. 'I told them all I knew, which was nothing of value. I told them that the plan was to take him out on a boat from the coast near Mangalore. But knowing you, I'm certain that's the last place you planned to take him to. So I really did not know where Shiva was and I do not know where he is now. I was tortured for nothing.'

'His name is Lakshman, not Shiva,' she muttered petulantly. 'Don't use that hateful name. To think that my own son would betray me.'

'You've said that before. Stop repeating yourself. It's becoming a bore. Did it go all right?'

Renuka took a deep breath. 'He got away.'

I laughed. 'Good, wonderful. One in the crotch for those cop bastards. Where is he now? Dubai? London? Montreal?'

Renuka hung her head and whispered: 'I don't know.'

'You don't know? What do you mean, you don't know. I thought you arranged everything.'

'I did.' Her head still hung down. 'I planned everything, down to the last detail. Even what clothes he must wear. He was to have been taken to a seaside village north of Cochin where a smugglers' boat would pick him up and take him to Dubai. All the necessary papers were fixed. Then, a plane to Geneva, by car across to Paris and then by plane to Montreal and Vancouver, where we have friends. My cousin in Dubai was to have accompanied him all the way.'

I stood up and grabbed her by the shoulders. 'What happened? Tell me, you miserable woman.'

She put her hands on my arms and looked up at me. Tears tricked down her cheeks. This was the first time I had seen her crying.

'He escaped. From me. From the men I had hired to take him to the west coast. He knocked out one man, held the rest up with the man's gun, tied them up and escaped. He did not want to run away. He ran back to his filthy, criminal Naxalite friends. He pinned a note on one of the men. 'Mother, father, I am going back to my people.' That was all that the note said. 'Oh, what shall I do now?' She was sobbing, gripping my arms hard, staring at me, fear in her eyes.

I smiled. I grinned. I laughed. I closed my eyes.

I whispered. 'My son' and the whisper was like a shout. 'My son. What a man. He's my son.'

Renuka shook me and slapped me. 'You filthy bastard,' she screamed. 'You're no father. You're a murderer. Your son goes to his death and you laugh like a madman. You're crazy. Oh, you bastard. You homicidal maniac.'

She ran out of the house.

I stood still, floating in the wonder of what my son had done.

'The age of the hero is come again,' I whispered in awe and gratitude.

# Chapter 17

*'Light thickens and the crow makes wing to the rooky wood'*

—'Macbeth', William Shakespeare

As I said 'the age of the hero is come again,' Dr Hekyll and Mr Jyde appeared before me for the last time.

They did not say anything. They just stood there smiling. And as they smiled, their images started fading.

'Don't go away. Stay with me,' I said.

'We are not going away, Bharat,' said Dr Hekyll. 'We will always be there, deep in your basal ganglia. After all, we are but splinters of your mind. But you won't be aware of us.'

Mr Jyde waved farewell. 'One request, before we leave,' he said. What is the answer to the question you posed in the first chapter'?

'Oh, yes,' I said. 'Thanks for reminding me. It is an old poem I wrote long ago. Let me read it out to you.'

I went to the bookshelf and took out the 'Collected Works of T S Eliot'. I took out a piece of paper that had been folded, opened and folded again many times I read out what I had written.

Love Song in a Waste Land

(Owed to Thomas Stearns Eliot).

*Tell me, should I, when I grow old*

*Wear the bottoms of my trousers rolled?*

*When I grow old,*

*Or so I'm told,*

*I must this material world disown,*

*Let wither what I've sown,*

*Give up the joys of Grihastashram,*

*And, worse, the nightly tot of rum.*

*They say I must the snowy mountains climb,*

*Drink cold water, not gin and lime.*

*In realms metaphysical I must travel,*

*Meditating strabismically on my navel.*

*Our great sages I do revere*

*But their recipe for Heaven is too severe*

*When I grow old*

*My trouser bottoms shall be rolled:*

*Rolled up firmly to the knees*

*As I seek the ineffable peace*

*Of dangling my feet in a swimming pool*

*As I ogle and drool*

*At bodies that bounce*

*As the girlies flounce*

*And squeal*

*And reveal*

*All: Youth*

*Is the Truth.*

*Datta, Damyata, Dayadhvam.*

*Waiter, a large double rum.*

*Om Shanti, Shanti, Shanti*

'Tamam Shud', said Dr Hekyll and Mr Jyde together.

And they disappeared.

And I became dull old Bharat Sharma once again.

*Krishna Krishna,* Indira Parthasarathy

Indira Parthasarathy's **Krishna Krishna** is an amalgam of the Harivamsam, Sri Bhagavatam, Vishnu Purana and the Mahabharata—a vehicle that carries the cultural and aesthetic themes into the literary discussion of the idea of Krishna.

ISBN : 978-81-8368-284-8

Price : 200 Pages : 246

*Star-Crossed,* Ashokamitran

Ashokamitran's **Star-crossed** is a novel about the world of Tamil cinema minus the glamour. It exposes the daily trials and tribulations of a cast of characters none too familiar to those who equate the world of celluloid with the proverbial dream factory.

ISBN : 978-81-8368-283-1

Price : 150 Pages : 144

*I, Ramaseshan,* Aadhavan

Aadhavan's **I, Ramaseshan** traces the emotional evolution of an adolescent growing into young adulthood. Written with humour and insight, the novel touches on the gaps in generations trying to understand each other.

ISBN : 978-81-8368-282-4

Price : 200 Pages : 216

*Love and Loss,* Jayakanthan

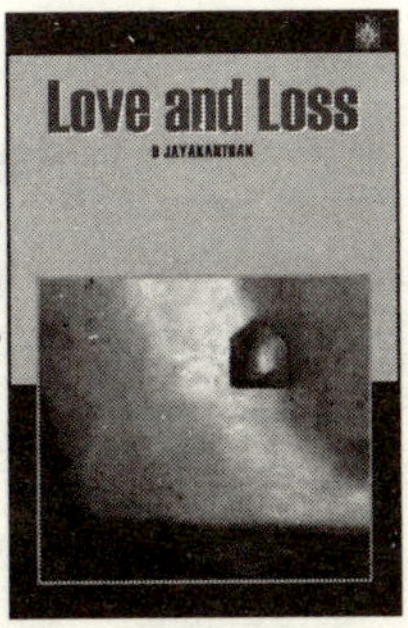


Jayakanthan's **Love and Loss** is a sensitive 'slice of life' story that explores the lives of Thangam, a construction worker and her son Chitti. The squalid slums of erstwhile Madras, now Chennai, form the grimy background to the tender drama of a woman trying to find an anchor to her life.

ISBN : 978-81-8368-285-5

Price : 150 Pages : 160

*A Home in the Sky,* Vaasanthi

Vaasanthi's **A Home in the Sky** is the story of the yearnings of an innocent child Raju, brutalised by a repressed, self-righteous father Sabhesan, who wallows in the misery of his self-imposed, rigid orthodoxy.

ISBN : 978-81-8368-351-7

Price : 200 Pages : 240

*Once an Actress,* Jayakanthan

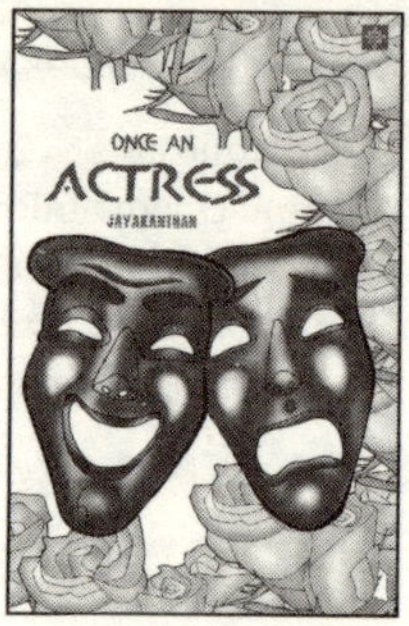


Jayakanthan's **Once an Actress** is about an intense interplay of emotions in a relationship punctuated by intolerance, separation and eventual reunion.

ISBN : 978-81-8368-352-4

Price : 200 Pages 232

*Wings in the Void,* Indira Parthasarathy

Indira Parthasarathy's **Wings in the Void** explores the wheeling and dealing, ambition and greed that rule the lives of countless upwardly mobile Indians caught up in the intrigues of the political and diplomatic circles of Delhi.

ISBN : 978-81-8368-353-1

Price : 200 Pages : 224

*Bridges,* Sivasankari

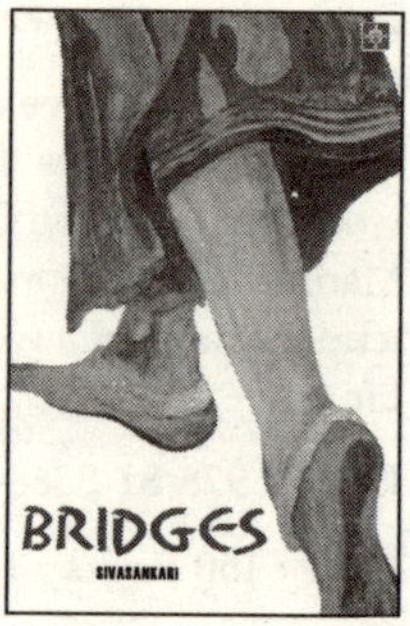


Sivasankari's **Bridges** is a saga of three generations of upper caste Tamil women. It gives the reader rare glimpses into customs and traditions typical of each period it covers—with an unjaundiced eye, great attention to detail, compassion and humour.

ISBN : 978-81-8368-354-8

Price : 200 Pages : 288

*Rishi Moolam,* Jayakanthan

Jayakanthan's two protagonists are helpless victims of psychological maladies. The author discusses themes such as suppressed libido and the Oedipus complex—areas Tamil writers generally dared not enter in the 1960s.

ISBN : 978-81-8368-382-1

Price : 150 Pages : 144

*Paper Flowers,* Aadhavan

Aadhavan's **Paper Flowers** explores the psyche of several individuals playing superficial roles in their daily encounters with life in a largely metropolitan setting. Insecurity and their sense of alienation prevent them from realising their potential. It is an outstanding representative of the emerging Tamil fiction of the 1970s.

ISBN : 978-81-8368-383-8

Price : 300 Pages : 408

*Today,* Ashokamitran

Ashokamitran's **Today** raises serious questions about the validity of the value systems governing our lives in an increasingly complex world. It is without doubt a trailblazer in post-modern Tamil literature.

ISBN : 978-81-8368-384-5

Price : 100 Pages : 88

*The Temple Elephant*, P S Sri

P S Sri's **The Temple Elephant** is narrated from the viewpoint of an elephant, it may be called a bestiary with a socio-political and spiritual message. Set against the backdrop of the British Raj, the novel takes us on an odyssey from the beautiful jungles of South India through the opulence of palace life to the serene simplicity of an ashram.

ISBN : 978-81-8368-385-2

Price : 100 Pages : 104

*Into this Heaven of Freedom,* Indira Parthasarathy

Set in New Delhi at the height of Indira Gandhi's reign, *Into this Heaven of Freedom* captures the intrigue, suspense, manoeuvring and one-upmanship that characterise politics.

ISBN : 978-81-8368-470-5

Price : 200 Pages : 216

*Where the Lord Sleeps,* Neela Padmanabhan

In this beautiful novel, Neela Padmanabhan has captured the soul of Trivandrum and laid it bare for us to see. Through the life of Anantan Nair—the humble hero of this novel—we experience the tragedy of the ancient regime of princely India and traditional Kerala society, caught in a whirl of vulgar modernisation.

ISBN : 978-81-8368-471-2

Price : 200 Pages : 240